WHAT THE LAKE KNOWS

WHAT THE LAKE KNOWS

DEVIENNE WEEKES

CONTENTS

One The Same Blue Sky ... 1

Two Down Into the Bones ... 9

Three What Surfaces ... 16

Four Postmarks ... 21

Five Fence Line ... 27

Six Undertow ... 34

Seven Loose Panels ... 41

Eight What Doesn't Move ... 46

Nine What Was Printed ... 50

Ten Contour Lines ... 55

Eleven Sightlines ... 61

Twelve Angles of Light ... 64

Thirteen Pressure Points ... 67

Fourteen Aftermath Logistics ... 73

Fifteen The Call Back ... 81

Sixteen Witness Lines ... 92

Seventeen First Entry ... 97

Eighteen Chain of Custody ... 103

Nineteen Holding Pattern ... 110

Twenty	Negative Space	114
Twenty One	Bare Ground	118
Twenty Two	Correction	123
Twenty Three	Held Ground	126
Twenty Four	Normal Hours	130
Twenty Five	Pressure Points	134
Twenty Six	Attention	138
Twenty Seven	Orientation	141
Twenty Eight	Official	144
Twenty Nine	Named	149
Thirty	After the Name	153
Thirty One	Moving Water	156
Thirty Two	After the Name	159
Thirty Three	Rising Water	163
Thirty Four	Swim Team	167
Thirty Five	Records	170
Thirty Six	Pressure	172
Thirty Seven	Narrowing	176
Thirty Eight	What People Knew	179
Thirty Nine	The Truth	182
Forty	Holding	188
Forty One	Memorial	198
Forty Two	Custody	204
Forty Three	Still Water	209

Forty Four Watching the Line   213

Forty Five Spring Work   217

Forty Six What Holds   222

Forty Seven What Stays   227

Forty Eight Commencement   230

Forty Nine The Edge   239

Notes   242

CHAPTER ONE

The Same Blue Sky

Emily Warren had been coming to Pine Valley Reservoir her entire life.

She had learned to swim there. Learned how to read the weather in the way the water changed color—green when storms pressed in, steel-gray before hail, bright and almost shallow-looking when the heat settled in for good. She learned which coves stayed warm longest in September, which rocks cut bare feet if you weren't careful, which stretches of shoreline you avoided because they dropped off too fast.

The lake had always been legible to her. Predictable, if you paid attention.

What she hadn't learned—what no one had ever taught her—was what the lake looked like when it gave something back.

Kate was sitting cross-legged on the living room floor when Emily grabbed her keys, her sketchbook open beside her. The page held the beginnings of something geometric—boxes, lines, angles that didn't quite resolve into a picture yet. One sneaker was kicked halfway off, the braid at the back of her head already unraveling.

"You're leaving?" Kate asked, without looking up.

"Picking up Grandpa," Emily said. "We're going to look at the reservoir."

Kate squinted. "At the empty lake?"

"It's still a lake," Emily said.

Kate made a face. "Empty lakes are haunted."

Emily smiled. "You say that about everything."

"That's because everything *is*," Kate said solemnly, then bent back over her drawing.

Emily watched her for a second longer than necessary. Kate had a way of stating things plainly—without irony, without softening—that adults tended to circle instead of confront. Emily sometimes wondered when that instinct got trained out of people. Or if it was something they gave up on purpose.

Her phone buzzed in her hand.

Grandma: You close?

Emily smiled before typing.

Emily: Just leaving the house.

Grandma: Good. Come in when you get here.

From the kitchen, her mom called, "Tell your grandparents we said hi."

"I will," Emily said, already halfway out the door.

* * *

Grandma and Grandpa's house sat a little back from the road, shaded by cottonwoods that dropped leaves everywhere except where you wanted them. Emily parked, cut the engine, and went up the steps without knocking. She never knocked. She'd never needed to.

The screen door creaked open.

Grandma was at the counter, folding parchment paper around something warm. She looked up when Emily came in, her face lighting in that easy, unguarded way that always made Emily feel like she'd arrived somewhere important—not just expected, but noticed.

"Morning, Emmy," Grandma said. "You're right on time."

She slid a paper-wrapped bundle into Emily's hands—still warm, smelling faintly of cinnamon and butter. A banana was tucked alongside it, secured with a folded napkin like it mattered.

"Breakfast," Grandma said. "For the road. Grandpa will forget if I don't send it with you."

Emily laughed. "He says he's not hungry."

"He's always not hungry until noon," Grandma said. "Then he's dramatic about it."

From the hallway, Grandpa's voice called, "I can hear you."

"That's the point," Grandma called back.

Emily leaned against the counter while Grandma tightened the twine. Up close, she smelled like coffee and clean cotton, familiar and grounding. There was something reassuring about how Grandma moved through space—efficient but gentle, like she believed care was something you did quietly, without expecting acknowledgment.

"Text when you get there," Grandma said, softer now. "And sunscreen. You know how he gets."

"I brought extra," Emily said.

Grandma's mouth curved—not proud, not anxious. Just certain. "I knew you would."

Grandpa appeared in the doorway, cap in hand. "You ready?"

"Been ready," Emily said, lifting the bundle. "Your breakfast says otherwise."

He grumbled, but he took it. Grandma smoothed his collar the way she always had—quick, affectionate, unthinking. The motion was so practiced it barely registered as movement.

"Don't rush," she said. "Look all you want."

Emily met her eyes. Something passed there—care, encouragement, a quiet kind of trust that felt heavier than reassurance.

"We will," Emily said.

* * *

Emily drove. Grandpa settled into the passenger seat, unwrapping the paper like it had surprised him.

"Your grandmother's going to run this town from the grave," he said, taking a bite.

Emily smiled. "Someone has to."

The road from Hillsborough unwound in slow curves, cutting through fields of sun-bleached grass and stands of lodgepole pine. Dust trailed behind them, rising like pale smoke before settling back into the land. The sky above them was the color of cut glass—deep, brilliant, endless. The kind of blue that made your chest tighten for reasons you couldn't quite explain.

Emily rested her elbow on the open window, the wind tugging at her braid.

"You sure you're up for this?" she asked.

Grandpa nodded. "Figured if I didn't go now, I never would."

"Everyone's talking about it," Emily said. "Coach Martin says someone found an old street sign poking out of the mud."

Grandpa snorted. "Coach Martin sees Elvis's ghost at the diner every Sunday."

Emily laughed, and the warm knot in her chest loosened. She loved Grandpa's dry humor. Loved the way he could be half-grumpy and half-soft at the same time.

But as the road descended toward the basin, his shoulders stiffened.

"It's really the lowest it's been?" she asked.

"Since they filled her," Grandpa said quietly. "They drained it on purpose. Repairs on the dam."

They didn't speak again until the reservoir came into view.

Or what was left of it.

A long, pale crater stretched wide and cracked, with only a narrow ribbon of water glinting far off toward the dam. The concrete boat ramp stood useless and high, leading down into nothing.

It was unsettling.

Like a secret unfolded.

Emily swallowed. "It looks like the moon."

"Mm," Grandpa said. "Never thought I'd see the bottom again."

* * *

They parked near the picnic shelter—the same one where Emily's family had spent summers and birthdays and ordinary afternoons that hadn't felt important until they were gone.

A soft breeze rattled the shelter's tin roof as they walked to the overlook.

And below them lay the valley.

Empty.

Quiet.

Laid bare.

"Oh," Emily whispered.

The reservoir floor was a patchwork of dried mud, shallow pools, and strange geometric shapes—rectangles, squares, faint lines crossing one another.

Foundations.

"What am I looking at?" she asked.

Grandpa leaned on the railing and exhaled slowly. "Evansville."

"The whole town?"

"What's left of it," he said. "The bones."

Emily couldn't look away. She'd heard stories all her life, but seeing it felt like reading something private—something that hadn't been meant to be found again. The kind of thing that made you lower your voice without realizing you'd done it.

Grandpa pointed things out as they stood there: the grocery, the barbershop, the Grange Hall.

"And that darker basin," he said eventually. "That was the Jennings place."

Emily followed his gaze. The water there looked heavier somehow—not darker from shadow, but weighted, as if it resisted light.

"That's where Clara lived," she said.

Grandpa nodded.

"What was she like?"

He took longer this time. His fingers curled against the railing, then loosened again.

"She paid attention," he said finally. "To people. To what they said and what they didn't. She laughed easy, but she noticed things. Talked about leaving, sure—but not like she was running. Like she expected to come back and find the world changed."

Emily hesitated. "What happened to her?"

Grandpa's jaw tightened. Not enough to be obvious. Enough to matter.

"That was the last time I saw her," he said. "Graduation night. After that—there were stories. Versions people found easier to hold."

The words settled in Emily's chest like something unfinished. Not grief exactly. More like a truth that had been set down before it was done.

"Water covers a lot," Grandpa added. "Always has."

Emily didn't argue. She was already beginning to understand that covering and forgetting weren't the same thing.

* * *

Emily met Zoe later at the gas station on Main. She went home. She asked questions no one could answer.

That night, Martha stopped by with a loaf of bread wrapped in a towel and stayed longer than usual.

"You look tired," Martha said, smoothing Emily's hair back the way she had when Emily was little.

"Long day," Emily said.

Martha studied her for a beat longer, then nodded. "Some days do that."

She hugged Emily before she left—warm, steady, familiar.

Emily watched her go and felt, inexplicably, like she was holding something fragile.

* * *

Sleep didn't come easily.

When it finally did, it felt more like falling into deep water than drifting off.

Emily dreamed of the valley—not the dry, cracked bowl she'd seen that afternoon, but the way it must have looked the night they flooded it. The roads were still there, but the lines were blurred, smeared by darkness and movement. Water lapped at fence posts and crept up porch steps.

A girl in a crimson graduation gown stood at the edge of the rising water, the hem already dark where it drank the lake. The braid down her back was damp, heavy.

Emily couldn't see her face.

"Don't," Emily tried to say, but her voice came out thick, like her mouth was full of river silt.

The girl didn't turn.

She stepped farther along the shore, where the ground sloped unevenly and the water climbed in shallow, quiet stages. Somewhere behind her, unseen, someone shouted—a voice Emily knew but couldn't place.

Ahead, the surface caught what little light it could, a thin shine like a blade.

The girl moved into it.

She didn't vanish violently.

She thinned.

One heartbeat she was there.

The next, she was only a distortion beneath the surface, a shape the water refused to keep sharp.

Emily reached for her.

The water closed over Emily's hand—cold, immediate—and tugged, hard, like undertow.

She gasped and jerked upright in bed.

The room was dark. Her T-shirt clung to her back with sweat, and her heart hammered like she'd been running hills.

From down the hall came a soft sound—Kate laughing briefly in her sleep, then settling again.

Emily pressed her palm to her chest, steadying her breath.

Through the open window, Pine Valley lay hidden beyond the dark line of pines, invisible but suddenly impossible to ignore. The night sky was a softer, deeper blue than the afternoon's blazing version, but it felt like the same sky all the same—watching, waiting.

Emily swallowed and whispered into the dark, "It was just a dream."

But it didn't feel like just anything.

It felt like the shoreline had shifted in the dark.

And something that should have stayed hidden had been covered instead.

CHAPTER TWO

Down Into the Bones

Morning didn't shake the dream loose.

She woke with her fist clenched in the bedsheet, heart still beating too fast. For a second, she half expected to find her shoes full of mud, her room damp, red fabric tangled around her ankles. Instead, there was only sunlight pressing through the curtains and the faint hum of the fridge down the hall.

It's just a dream, she told herself.

But when she closed her eyes, she saw the crimson gown again—dark at the hem, heavy with water.

"Em? You awake?" her dad called from the kitchen.

"Yeah," she croaked, swinging her legs out of bed.

Her muscles ached pleasantly from yesterday. Not the walking, exactly—she hadn't realized until she'd gone to sleep how much tension she'd been carrying in her shoulders. She stretched until her spine cracked and told herself that meant she was fine.

In the bathroom mirror, her eyes looked shadowed, like something hadn't finished leaving her. She stared at herself for a moment, then grabbed her brush and pulled her hair into its usual tight braid.

"Okay," she told her reflection. "No more lake dreams."

Her reflection didn't argue.

Down the hall, Kate's door stood half open. Music spilled out—loud, dramatic, the kind of song that made everything feel important even if nothing was happening.

Kate appeared in the doorway a minute later in an oversized sweat-shirt and shorts, hair doing whatever it wanted.

"You're up," Emily said.

Kate shrugged. "Mom says I have to 'fix my schedule' before fresh-man orientation." She made air quotes. "Apparently sleeping past nine is how you ruin your life."

"You'll survive," Emily said.

Kate studied her, eyes narrowing. "You look like you lost a fight."

"I didn't."

"With what?"

"Nothing."

Kate grinned. "Haunted."

"Go haunt your cereal," Emily said.

Kate laughed and wandered toward the kitchen.

* * *

Both of Emily's parents were at the table—her dad with coffee and the newspaper, her mom scrolling her phone between bites of toast. The kitchen smelled like eggs and butter and dish soap, the ordinary kind of morning that was supposed to make everything feel normal.

Kate dropped into a chair and stole a piece of toast from her dad's plate.

"Hey," he protested.

"Fuel," Kate said.

Emily sat and stared at her eggs longer than necessary.

"You're up early," her dad said. "Thought you'd sleep till noon."

"Senior summer," her mom added. "Enjoy it while you can."

"Can't wait," Emily said dryly.

Her dad smiled. "We aim to inspire."

Emily pushed her fork through the eggs without eating.

"Grandpa okay this morning?" she asked.

Her mom glanced up. "I talked to your grandma. He slept fine. Why?"

"He just seemed... shaken," Emily said.

Her dad nodded slowly. "Wouldn't you be? Going back to the place where your whole childhood used to be?"

Emily's dad had grown up in Montana, but not here. He'd met Mom at Montana State, and Hillsborough had always sounded like "home" when Mom said it—until Emily realized how much the word could hide.

Emily nodded, but that wasn't what she was thinking about.

"He talked about Clara," Emily said.

The table went quiet. Not abruptly—just enough to notice.

"Not much," Emily added quickly. "Just... graduation day. He said the sky was this same blue."

Her mom set her phone down carefully. "So he's thinking about her again."

"Again?" Emily asked.

"There was a time," her dad said, choosing his words, "when he mentioned her now and then. When you were younger. Before your grandma asked him not to."

Kate looked between them, alert but silent.

Emily swallowed. "Do you think she drowned?"

Her parents exchanged a glance.

"They searched," her mom said finally. "But graduation night was chaos."

Her dad nodded. "Your mom's told me about that night, and I've heard it from enough people to know how it went. They'd started flooding the valley. The water rose in stages, not all at once—but people were celebrating, packing, leaving. Equipment everywhere. By nightfall, flashlights didn't help much."

Emily's stomach tightened.

"So no one saw."

"No one who could be sure," her dad said.

"But it wasn't an accident," Emily said. The words surprised her with how firm they sounded. "The flooding was planned. They knew the water was coming."

Her dad nodded. "Yes. It was planned."

Planned.

The word sat wrong.

Kate pushed back from the table. "I'm going to go be productive," she announced. She grabbed an apple, then paused.

"If you're... thinking about weird stuff," she said to Emily, suddenly awkward, "you can tell me."

Emily blinked.

Kate shrugged. "I'm not a baby. I'm basically a high schooler."

Emily smiled. "I know."

Kate nodded once and left.

***

By ten, the heat was already rising off the pavement. Hillsborough in summer smelled like dust, pine sap, and gasoline from the two-pump station on Main.

Emily pulled on cutoffs and a tank top, laced her trail shoes, and filled a water bottle. On impulse, she grabbed the cheap digital camera she'd found at a thrift store—a clunky silver thing that made everything feel harder to erase.

Her phone buzzed.

A text from Grandma.

Grandma: Morning, Emmy.

Grandma: Your grandpa's acting like he's fine. Which means he isn't.

Grandma: You okay?

Emily stared at the screen.

Emily: I'm okay. Just thinking about yesterday.

Emily: Tell Grandpa I'm glad we went.

A pause.

Grandma: He was glad too.

Grandma: Just be careful down there. The county's starting work on the dam early.

Emily's pulse jumped.

So it wasn't later. It was now.

Emily: I will.

She slid her phone into her pocket before she could think too hard about why the message felt like both a warning and a comfort.

"Where are you headed?" her mom called.

"Just out," Emily said. "Thought I'd take pictures."

Her mom frowned. "Stay away from the reservoir."

"I'm not going in," Emily said. "Just the overlook. I'll text."

Her mom hesitated, then nodded. "Okay. But text."

"I will."

Mostly.

* * *

The drive back to Pine Valley felt different alone.

Yesterday it had been full of Tom's memories—names, places, the way his voice shifted when he didn't want to finish a thought. Today it was just heat and sky, still that same impossible blue.

Emily parked by the picnic shelter and sat for a moment with her hands on the wheel.

New signs had been posted.

CAUTION: UNSTABLE GROUND

DAM MAINTENANCE — AREA RESTRICTED

HISTORICAL SITE — DO NOT REMOVE ARTIFACTS

Someone had scrawled beneath them in marker: *Too late.*

Emily should have turned around.

Instead she grabbed her camera and walked to the overlook.

The basin looked harsher in midday light. The remaining ribbon of water glared like metal.

Her phone buzzed.

Mom: You there?
Emily: Yep. Just the overlook.
For now.

The boat ramp jutted out above the valley floor, a narrow path worn beside it by curiosity. Emily hesitated, then started down.

The slope was steeper than it looked. Dust slid under her shoes, but she kept her footing. The heat pressed in; the breeze off the water cooled the sweat at her neck.

At the bottom, the mud was firm in places and soft in others. Shoe prints marked the surface.

The foundations rose higher from this angle.

Emily stepped into the outline of Whitman's Grocery, then moved on. Barbershop. Grange Hall. Tile half-buried in dirt.

She crouched, brushed it clean, and left it where it was.

Then she saw it.

The Jennings place.

The water there was darker. Still.

Emily stopped at the edge.

"Hi, Clara," she whispered.

Her voice sounded too loud.

She crouched and scanned the depression. Something rusted lay just beneath the waterline—too straight to be natural.

Her heart sped up.

Cellar, her mind supplied.

She told herself not to jump to conclusions.

But when she eased down the slope and brushed away silt, her fingers found edges.

A frame.

A door.

Emily sat back hard, mud squelching under her.

"Okay," she whispered. "Okay."

She didn't open it.

Not today.

She climbed back up, wiped her hands on her shorts, and took one photo.

Just in case.

The image looked ordinary.

Her skin still prickled.

Emily turned toward the ramp, knowing one thing with absolute certainty:

Whatever had happened here hadn't been finished.

And she had just stepped into it.

CHAPTER THREE

What Surfaces

Emily didn't tell anyone about the door.

Not her mom, not Zoe, not even Grandpa Tom when he called that evening and asked if she'd "enjoyed the sunshine." She said yes, because it was easier than explaining the way the valley had followed her home, the way it had settled into her bones like a held breath that hadn't yet decided whether to release.

That night, she lay on her bed with the cheap digital camera resting on her stomach, staring up at the ceiling fan as it clicked unevenly overhead. The sound was familiar, comforting—something she'd fallen asleep to a hundred times before. Tonight, it felt too loud.

The image from the Jennings' foundation stayed sharp in her mind.

Ordinary.

Empty.

Safe-looking.

Which made it worse.

She rolled onto her side and turned the camera on again. The small screen glowed pale blue in the dark as she scrolled through the photos she'd taken that afternoon: Whitman's Grocery, the long stretch of what had once been Main Street, the corner of blue-and-white tile half-swallowed by dirt. Each image felt flat, stripped of the pressure she'd felt standing there, like the valley had been holding something back just for her.

Then she reached the last photo.

The Jennings' place.

At first glance, it was exactly what she remembered—cracked concrete, weeds, a dark oval of water caught in the foundation's corner. She leaned closer, heart slowing, then tightening.

The shadow wasn't where she remembered it being.

It had shifted—angled closer to the corner where the metal frame lay buried beneath the surface.

"That's impossible," she whispered.

She zoomed in. The image blurred into pixels, then sharpened again. The water's surface was smooth. Still. But along the edge of the shadow ran a line—straight in a way water never was.

Emily shut the camera off and set it face-down on the nightstand, as if it might accuse her if she kept looking.

Sleep came in pieces.

She dreamed of water again, but this time it was draining—rushing away in long, echoing gulps, like something being pulled free. As the water receded, something pale emerged beneath it. Wood, maybe. Hands.

Something was knocking.

Not on a door.

From beneath one.

Emily woke with a sharp gasp. For a moment she couldn't tell if the sound had followed her out of the dream. Her room was dark and still, the fan ticking overhead.

Then came a soft tap at the window.

"Em," Zoe hissed. "Open up."

Emily shoved the curtain aside and slid the window open. Zoe stood below, flashlight clutched in one hand, her hair pulled into a messy knot like she hadn't bothered convincing herself this was a good idea.

"You are going to get me grounded for life," Emily whispered.

Zoe grinned. "Worth it."

"No."

"Before you say no," Zoe said quickly, lowering her voice, "my brother says they're fencing the reservoir tomorrow. Real fencing. Cameras, maybe. And you don't strike me as the kind of person who lets things go once they start bothering you."

Emily hesitated.

She thought of the photo. The shadow. The straight line beneath the water.

"Five minutes," she said. "If it feels wrong, we leave."

Zoe's grin softened. "Deal."

* * *

They parked farther down the road and cut through the pines instead of using the main lot. The night air was cooler, heavy with damp earth and sap. Crickets buzzed unevenly, their rhythm breaking and restarting like something unsettled.

The moon hung low, turning the basin into a pale bowl of shadow.

From above, the valley didn't look empty.

It looked watched.

Someone had left fresh flowers near the overlook railing—wild daisies, already wilting, stems snapped short. No card. No name.

They picked their way down slowly, flashlights off, letting moonlight guide them. The foundations blurred together in the dark, their edges softened, the grid of the old town less certain. The thin ribbon of remaining water reflected the moon like a broken mirror.

When the Jennings' foundation came into view, Zoe stopped.

"Oh," she breathed. "That one's different."

Emily nodded. "Yeah."

The pool looked darker at night, swallowing light instead of reflecting it. The weeds around it stirred faintly, though there was no wind.

Emily crouched and pointed. "Right there. Under the waterline."

Zoe squinted. "You're sure?"

"I'm sure enough."

They stood in silence.

Then—

A hollow sound echoed up through the foundation.

Not loud.

Just enough to feel.

Zoe sucked in a breath. "Okay—no. That could've just been the ground settling."

She didn't sound convinced.

"They drained a whole lake," she added quickly. "Stuff shifts. It happens."

Emily's pulse roared in her ears. She waited.

The sound didn't come again.

The pool went still. The weeds stopped moving.

Emily let out a breath she hadn't realized she was holding.

"Clara didn't run away," she whispered—not because she was certain, but because the words felt heavier than doubt.

Zoe swallowed. "We should go."

Emily nodded.

They didn't run. They didn't look back.

They just left.

* * *

Halfway up the slope, a voice carried down from the boat ramp.

"Hey—careful down there!"

Two figures stood silhouetted against the sky.

"The ground's soft," one called. "Easy to get stuck."

"We're leaving," Emily called back.

She didn't look behind her again.

* * *

At home, Emily lay awake long after Zoe had gone, staring at the dark outline of her ceiling. Evansville names drifted through her thoughts—Warren, Jennings, Callahan, Whitman. Names she knew. Names she didn't. Families who had left flowers. Families who still watched the water.

Her phone buzzed.

Zoe: You okay?

Emily: Yeah. Just thinking.

She set the phone down and pressed her palm flat against her chest, steadying her breath.

There was something under that door.

She didn't know yet what it was.

But she knew this much—

It wasn't finished being found.

CHAPTER FOUR

Postmarks

Emily didn't go looking for the letters. They found her the way small-town things always did—through half-finished conversations and the way people's voices dropped when she stepped too close.

At the hardware store, the clerk slid a stack of flyers across the counter with her change:

DAM MAINTENANCE UPDATE, HISTORICAL SOCIETY MEETING, NO TRESPASSING — UNSTABLE GROUND.

Someone had circled *Evansville artifacts* in pen.

Outside, Zoe was leaning against Emily's truck, gnawing on a Slim Jim like it was a personal problem.

"You heard about the letters?" Zoe asked.

Emily paused. "What letters?"

Zoe's eyes lit. "Okay, so—apparently, there are undelivered letters from Evansville. Like, boxes of them. People are saying the Harpers still have them."

Emily frowned. "Why would they?"

Zoe lowered her voice. "Because Blake's great-grandpa was the postmaster back then. And Earl—Blake's grandpa—is still alive. So... nothing ever really got revisited."

Emily felt something tighten in her chest. "Where did you hear this?"

"My aunt," Zoe said. "She volunteers with the historical society. She's been saying it's going to come up."

Emily nodded once. "Do you know where Blake is?"

Zoe studied her. "You're going to ask him."

Emily didn't answer.

That was answer enough.

* * *

Blake was loading folding chairs into the back of a pickup behind the historical society when Emily pulled into the lot.

He didn't look surprised to see her. If anything, he looked like he'd noticed her truck and decided not to react yet.

Emily crossed the gravel.

"Hey," she said.

Blake glanced up, then back to the chair in his hands. "Hey."

Not unfriendly. Not inviting.

"I heard something," Emily said.

That made him pause. He set the chair down carefully and straightened.

"About what?"

"Letters," she said. "From Evansville."

Blake's eyes flicked toward the open door of the building, where volunteers were moving chairs and talking over one another. Then back to her.

"Where did you hear that?"

"Is it true?" Emily asked.

A beat passed.

Then Blake nodded once. "Yeah."

The word landed heavier than a denial would have.

"Why do you have them?" Emily asked.

"We don't," Blake said. "Not like you're thinking."

"Then who does?"

Blake exhaled slowly. "This isn't really a public conversation."

Emily followed his glance toward the doorway. "Okay. Then where does it happen?"

He studied her for a second—not weighing courage, just intent.

"My grandpa's place," he said finally. "I'm heading back there anyway."

"You're not inviting me," Emily said.

"No," Blake said evenly. "I'm setting boundaries."

"What kind?"

"You don't open anything. You don't take pictures. And if he tells you to leave, you leave."

Emily nodded. "That's fair."

Blake looked mildly surprised she didn't argue.

"Why do you care?" he asked—not accusing, just asking.

Emily didn't soften it. "Because Clara Jennings disappeared and everyone here acts like that's settled."

Blake's jaw tightened—not defensively. Protectively.

"Careful," he said quietly.

"With what?"

"With assuming silence means nothing," Blake said. "Sometimes it just means people got used to living with it."

Emily held his gaze. "And sometimes it means they decided what mattered more than the truth."

Blake looked away first.

"Get in your truck," he said. "I don't want this turning into something."

* * *

Earl Harper Jr.'s house sat at the edge of town, where pavement gave way to scrub and pine. The yard was tidy without being precious. Wind chimes clicked softly under the porch eave.

Blake let them in without knocking.

Inside, the house smelled faintly of coffee and clean wood. Earl sat in a recliner by the window, a book open on his lap. He looked up as they entered.

"Blake," he said. Then his gaze moved to Emily. "Emily Warren."

Emily swallowed. "Hello, Mr. Harper."

"Earl's fine."

Blake hovered briefly, then moved toward the kitchen. "Coffee," he muttered.

Earl watched him go, something softening in his expression, then turned back to Emily.

"You're here about the letters," he said.

Emily nodded. "Yes."

Earl closed his book. "They're in the back."

Blake returned, set a mug on the table, and avoided Emily's eyes.

"Blake," Earl said calmly. "Show her. Then give us a minute."

Blake hesitated, then nodded.

* * *

The room at the back of the house wasn't a bedroom. It was an office.

File cabinets. Shelves. Binders. Three banker's boxes taped shut, labeled neatly in black marker.

EVANSVILLE

Blake stood by the door.

"My great-grandfather was the postmaster," he said quietly. "Not my grandpa. Earl's dad."

Emily nodded, the timeline clicking into place.

"And your grandpa knew," she said.

"Yes."

"And didn't change it."

Blake looked away. "No."

Emily stepped closer to the boxes. The tape was brittle. The cardboard softened at the corners.

"You said I couldn't open them," she said.

"You can't."

She took a breath—and stepped back.

"Okay."

Something eased in Blake's shoulders.

He turned off the light and closed the door.

* * *

Back in the living room, Earl watched her carefully.

"You didn't open them," he said.

"No."

"Good."

Emily sat on the edge of the couch. "Why keep them?"

Earl looked toward the window. "My father believed in order. He thought if you didn't stir things up, they'd settle."

"They don't," Emily said quietly. "They just get quiet."

Earl met her gaze.

"By the time I could've changed it," he said, "not changing it had already become its own decision."

Emily felt the weight of that.

"Did you know Clara?" she asked.

"Yes."

"Do you know what happened to her?"

Earl looked down at his hands. "I didn't see it happen."

"But you think you know."

Earl lifted his eyes, tired but steady. "I think some truths don't come with proof. They come with consequences."

Blake shifted near the doorway.

Earl's voice softened. "You're asking questions that don't stay polite, Emily Warren. Be careful what you decide to carry forward."

Emily stood. "Thank you for showing me."

Earl nodded once.

Outside, the air felt cooler.

Blake paused on the porch. "Don't push him," he said. "He won't bend. He'll just close."

"I'm not trying to break him," Emily said.

Blake shook his head. "That's how it happens anyway."

* * *

Martha was waiting at the kitchen table when Emily got home, tea steaming between her hands.

"You look like you've been somewhere heavy," she said.

"I went to Earl Harper's."

Martha's fingers tightened around the mug. "And?"

"He has letters," Emily said. "Undelivered ones."

Martha nodded. "I figured."

"Did you ever write one?"

"Yes."

"Did you send it?"

"No."

Martha reached across the table and covered Emily's hand.

"Some things," she said softly, "were set aside because no one knew where they belonged anymore."

Emily nodded.

It still felt right.

And still incomplete.

* * *

That night, Emily lay awake listening to the ordinary sounds of summer.

The letters.

The lake.

The door.

Not ghosts. Not curses.

Just people.

And the places where they decided to stop.

CHAPTER FIVE

Fence Line

The next morning, the town woke up like it had agreed on something.

Emily noticed it in the small ways first—her mom moving through the kitchen with the radio turned down, like sound itself might make things worse; the way the coffee maker clicked off and no one commented on the silence that followed; the careful way the curtains were pulled back, just enough to let light in without committing to seeing too much of the street.

Kate paused in the doorway, watching Emily with narrowed eyes, as if she were trying to solve something without all the information. She'd been doing that more lately—standing still while other people moved, paying attention to what didn't get said.

Then Emily's phone buzzed.

Zoe: they're fencing it today. like actual fence.

Emily read the message once. Then again. Then she set her phone face-down on the table, as if the words might spread if she left them exposed.

Kate slid into the chair across from her, dragging a bowl of cereal with more force than necessary. Milk sloshed dangerously close to the rim.

"You look like you're thinking too hard," Kate said.

"That's not a thing."

"It is," Kate said. "Dad says it about Mom when she starts cleaning the same counter over and over."

Emily smiled faintly. "What do you want?"

Kate shrugged, spoon tapping the edge of the bowl in a nervous rhythm. "Are you going back down there?"

Emily reached for her coffee. The pause was small. Not even a second.

But it was enough.

Kate's eyebrows lifted. "Knew it."

"Kate."

"I'm not a kid," Kate said. "I'm starting high school. I hear things."

Emily's stomach tightened. "Like what?"

Kate hesitated, eyes dropping to the cereal, then back up again. "Like that girl. Clara."

The spoon stilled.

Emily kept her voice even. "Where did you hear that name?"

Kate shrugged, but this time it was smaller. Defensive. "People say it and then stop talking. Like it's something you're not supposed to ask about."

That felt right. Uncomfortably so.

"Clara Jennings went missing," Emily said. "A long time ago."

Kate's eyes widened. "Missing like... never came back?"

"Yes."

Kate leaned back in her chair, suddenly quieter, the edge gone from her posture. "And you're trying to figure out what happened."

Emily shook her head. "I'm trying to understand why people stopped asking."

Kate thought about that. She always did—turned ideas over like stones, testing their weight.

Then she nodded once. "Okay."

Emily studied her sister. Kate still looked fourteen in the unguarded light of the kitchen—long limbs that hadn't quite learned where to settle, elbows sharp against the table edge, shoulders narrow beneath the oversized sweatshirt she'd stolen from Emily months ago. In the slant of late-afternoon sun, her auburn hair caught and held the light, copper bright against the dim room. Her eyes—green and unsettled, like the lake after a storm—felt older than the rest of her. Kate had a way of walking straight toward things other people circled—not because she was brave, exactly, but because she hadn't yet learned what made people uncomfortable. She didn't recognize the social warning signs, the invisible fences that adults built and maintained without thinking.

Emily didn't want to be the one to teach her.

Her phone buzzed again.

Grandpa: You around? Historical society's short a couple people down by the dam. Could use a runner if you're free.

Emily stared at the message.

An errand.

A task.

Nothing more than that.

She stood, already reaching for her keys.

"Tell Mom I'll be back later," she said.

Kate looked up. "Where are you going?"

"Somewhere boring."

Kate snorted. "Liar."

Emily paused at the door. "Kate—stay out of it."

Kate crossed her arms. "Fine. But if the lake eats you, I'm not helping."

Emily left before she could laugh, before the tension in her chest could turn into something heavier.

* * *

Grandpa was parked at the turnout near the dam access road, leaning against his truck with a clipboard tucked under one arm and a paper cup of coffee in the other. A volunteer badge hung crookedly from his shirt pocket, the plastic scratched from years of reuse.

When Emily pulled in, he lifted the coffee in greeting.

"There you are," he said.

Emily got out of her truck. "You're volunteering now?"

Grandpa snorted. "Don't tell anyone. I have a reputation."

He handed her the clipboard. "They need someone to run messages, keep people from wandering where they shouldn't, and make sure nobody decides a piece of history fits in their pocket."

Emily skimmed the list. Fencing panels. Signage. Water. Names she recognized and a few she didn't.

"The fence seems dramatic," she said.

Grandpa looked out toward the basin.

The reservoir, drawn down for repairs, lay open and exposed. Foundations cut clean lines through the dirt. The shape of Evansville was clearer than it had been in years—too clear, like something uncovered before anyone had decided what to do with it.

"They're not worried about drama," Grandpa said. "They're worried about liability."

Emily nodded.

"Soft ground," he added. "Curious people."

"And the fence fixes that?"

"It slows the ones who care what they look like," Grandpa said.

Emily laughed once, surprised by the bluntness of it.

Grandpa smiled at the sound. "That's my girl."

The words warmed her—and unsettled her—all at once. Praise felt heavier lately. Like it came with expectations she hadn't agreed to yet.

"Come on," Grandpa said. "Take this over to Miller."

Emily nodded and headed down the gravel path toward the workers. The air smelled like dust and sun-warmed metal. Fence panels rattled as they were lifted into place, the sound echoing oddly across the basin, sharp and hollow.

As she walked, she felt it again—not watched.

Remembered.

A place registering attention after a long time without it. As if the ground itself had grown unused to being noticed and didn't know what to do with the weight of eyes.

"You Miller?" she asked.

A man in a hard hat nodded, took the clipboard, scanned it. "You with the historical society?"

"Sort of," Emily said.

"That counts," he replied, already turning away. "West edge first. County wants it hard to climb."

Emily nodded and stepped back, the work moving around her with practiced efficiency.

Her gaze drifted—just briefly—toward the Jennings foundation.

The shallow pool beside it was dark and still, untouched by wind. The surface didn't ripple like the others. It held.

Emily forced herself to look away.

* * *

By midday, the fence was half finished.

Metal panels rattled in the wind. New signs flashed white in the sun:

NO TRESPASSING
UNSTABLE GROUND
AUTHORIZED PERSONNEL ONLY

They looked official. Final. Like words that expected to be obeyed.

Emily ferried water bottles, relayed messages, checked off lists. Ordinary work. The kind that kept your hands busy while your mind wandered somewhere less manageable.

But the air felt tight, like the town had drawn a line and was waiting to see who crossed it.

People gathered at the overlook despite the heat—neighbors, tourists, a few locals pretending not to care. They stood just far enough back to claim compliance, leaning forward to see as much as they could without stepping over.

Emily caught fragments as she passed.

"Probably safer this way."

"Can't have kids falling in."

"Best to leave it alone."

Leave it alone.

She wondered how long people had been telling themselves that.

Grandpa joined her while she was stacking cones near the access road.

"You holding up?" he asked.

"Yeah."

He nodded, satisfied. He didn't look at her like someone waiting for a confession. Just like someone checking in.

"I went to see Earl Harper," Emily said before she could stop herself.

Grandpa paused. Just long enough to register the name.

"When?"

"Yesterday."

He considered that. "Earl's been around a long time," he said finally. "That doesn't mean he's right about everything."

Emily watched him carefully. He wasn't probing. Wasn't asking what Earl had said or why she'd gone. He was placing the name where it belonged—on the edge of relevance, not at the center.

"Just help out," Grandpa added. "And watch your footing."

That was all.

No warning. No suspicion.

No attempt to redirect her.

Emily nodded.

Grandpa handed her a granola bar. "Eat."

She took it, the wrapper crinkling too loudly in the stillness.

"After this," he said, voice lower, "we head back together."

Emily nodded again.

He squeezed her shoulder once before walking away—firm, grounding, a reminder of presence rather than control.

Emily stood there with the fence line in front of her and the weight of the town behind her.

The panels rattled.
The foundations sat in the sun.
Nothing hidden. Nothing resolved.
Just a boundary drawn too late.
And the growing understanding that someone, years ago, had decided where that boundary should go—and who it was meant to protect.

CHAPTER SIX

Undertow

The first text came while Emily was standing in line at the grocery store, her phone balanced against a carton of eggs and a loaf of bread that kept sliding toward the edge of the counter.

She nudged the bread back with her wrist and shifted her weight, aware of the heat pooling between her shoulders. The air inside the store felt thicker than usual, stale with bleach and overripe fruit. Somewhere behind her, a freezer hummed too loudly. Ahead of her, a man argued in a low, irritated voice with the cashier about a coupon that had expired last month.

Emily let her eyes unfocus, letting the noise blur into something manageable.

Her phone vibrated once.

She almost ignored it. Almost.

Unknown Number: Some things don't stay buried just because they're quiet.

Emily stared at the screen.

Her heart didn't race.

It stilled.

The words didn't feel threatening. They didn't arrive sharp or aggressive. They felt... placed. Like something set down carefully rather than thrown. She read it again, slower this time, as if cadence might reveal intent—where the emphasis landed, what kind of voice had shaped it.

Some things don't stay buried.

The phrase carried weight without urgency. Observation, not warning. Fact, not fear.

The cashier cleared her throat.

Emily blinked, startled by how far she'd drifted. She slid her card into the reader, took the bag when it was handed to her, and walked out into the heat with the phone still in her hand.

Outside, the parking lot shimmered. Tires hummed against asphalt. Someone laughed near the propane exchange like it was any other morning. A pickup rumbled past with its windows down, country music spilling out in a careless rush.

Normal life, continuing.

Emily unlocked her truck and slid inside, shutting the door hard enough to feel it reverberate through her arms. The air was thick and unmoving. She rolled down the window but didn't start the engine.

She didn't respond.

She didn't block the number.

She turned the phone face-down in the cup holder and rested her forehead against the steering wheel until the heat soaked through her skin, until the physical discomfort gave her something solid to hold onto.

"You don't get to do that," she muttered into the empty cab. "You don't get to say something like that and disappear."

But whoever it was already had.

She flipped down the visor and caught her reflection in the small mirror—familiar, unchanged. Same eyes. Same mouth. Nothing about her face gave away the way something had shifted, subtle and irrevocable.

She started the truck.

*　*　*

She drove without direction at first.

Past the diner, its windows crowded with late-morning regulars hunched over coffee cups. Past the Pine Valley turnoff. She slowed there without meaning to, her foot easing off the gas as if the road itself had asked her to hesitate.

She didn't turn.

Instead, she kept going, following the stretch of highway that ran farther than most people bothered with once there was no reason to. The hills rose gently on either side, trees thinning just enough to let the sky press down—wide, pale, unbroken.

No radio. No chatter.

Just wind, tires, and the steady hum of the road beneath her.

Emily pulled over where gravel replaced pavement and shut off the engine.

Dust settled around the truck in a slow halo. She took her phone out again, turned it over, half-expecting the screen to light the moment she acknowledged it.

Nothing.

She exhaled.

The quiet out here was different. Not peaceful. Just less interrupted. It didn't soften anything—it gave her thoughts more room to stretch.

People in Pine Valley didn't usually communicate like this. They left notes on counters. Passed messages through other people. Let information travel softened, reshaped, diluted by repetition.

This had cut straight through all of that.

She stared out at the hills until the tension in her shoulders dulled into something heavier, more manageable. Then she angled the truck back toward town.

* * *

That afternoon, Grandma stopped by.

She knocked—soft, habitual—but didn't wait long before opening the door like she already knew she'd be welcome.

"I was in the neighborhood," she said, holding up a small paper sack. "Your mom said you were out earlier. I thought you might not have eaten."

Emily took the bag. It was warm, the paper creased where Grandma's fingers had held it. The smell—cheese, bread, something faintly sweet—rose immediately.

"Thanks," Emily said.

Grandma stepped inside, her gaze sweeping the room the way it always did—quick, affectionate, cataloging without judgment. A book left open on the couch. Shoes kicked slightly out of place by the door. The faint hum of the refrigerator.

She sat at the table without being asked.

Emily poured tea, the kettle clicking off too loudly in the quiet. Grandma wrapped her hands around the mug when it was set in front of her, breathing in the steam like she was grounding herself as much as Emily was.

"You look like you're carrying something," Grandma said gently.

Not accusing. Not curious.

Just observant.

Emily hesitated. She'd been doing that more lately—pausing at the edge of sentences, deciding what weight she could set down without breaking anything.

"I got a weird text," she said finally.

Grandma's hands stilled around the mug. Not stiffening. Just pausing.

"From who?"

"I don't know."

A beat passed. Grandma nodded once, accepting the uncertainty rather than pushing against it.

"Do you want to show me?" she asked.

Emily shook her head. "Not yet."

Grandma didn't ask why. She took a slow sip of tea instead, giving the moment room.

"That's okay," she said. "Some things need a minute before they're ready to be shared."

Emily studied her. Grandma's face was familiar in the deepest sense—lined by years of smiling and worrying and being useful to people who leaned on her without realizing it. There was comfort in that steadiness.

And something else. Something careful.

"Did you ever feel like this town remembers things wrong?" Emily asked. "Or... not wrong. Just unevenly."

Grandma considered that. She didn't answer right away.

"Yes," she said finally.

"Like some people get remembered," Emily continued, "and some just... get absorbed?"

Grandma looked out the window toward the tree line, where the hills hid the basin beyond them. A cloud passed, shifting the light across her face.

"Places remember better than people," she said. "But people decide what to listen to."

Emily nodded. That felt right. It also felt incomplete.

"What about when people decide not to listen?" Emily asked.

Grandma smiled faintly. "That's usually a group decision."

Emily frowned. "So it's not an accident."

"No," Grandma said gently. "It's maintenance."

The word settled between them.

Grandma reached out then, smoothing the paper sack as if straightening something that didn't need it. "Most towns survive by narrowing their stories," she said. "It's not cruelty. It's practicality. Too many open threads and people stop sleeping."

Emily thought of the text. The careful phrasing. The way it had arrived without asking permission.

"Does that make it right?" she asked.

Grandma met her gaze. "It makes it understandable."

Emily didn't like that answer. But she didn't argue with it either.

Grandma stood, moved behind her, and pressed a brief kiss to the crown of her head—steady, grounding, asking nothing in return.

"Eat," she said. "And don't stay up too late."

Emily smiled despite herself. "You sound like Mom."

Grandma's mouth curved. "We trade notes."

After she left, Emily sat alone at the table longer than necessary, the warmth from the paper sack fading slowly. She didn't reread the text. She didn't delete it.

She folded the bag neatly and set it aside.

* * *

That night, Emily lay awake listening to the low hum of summer—crickets outside the window, distant traffic on the highway, Kate turning over in her sleep down the hall.

The house felt settled. Unaware of the tension threading through her chest.

Her phone buzzed.

Unknown Number: People told themselves it was an ending. It wasn't.

Emily sat up, the mattress creaking softly beneath her.

Emily: Who is this?

The reply didn't come right away.

The waiting felt deliberate.

Unknown Number: Someone who remembers what the water looked like before it came all the way in.

Emily swallowed.

Emily: Why tell me?

Three dots appeared. Disappeared. Appeared again.

Unknown Number: Because you're asking questions no one else is anymore.

Emily stared at the words until her eyes burned.

Emily: About Clara?

The pause stretched long enough to hurt.

Then—
Unknown Number: About everyone.

Emily's chest tightened.

Not fear.

Recognition.

Emily: What do you want?

The phone stayed dark long enough that she almost set it down.

Then—

Unknown Number: For you not to carry what isn't yours.

Emily exhaled shakily.

Emily: Then stop texting me.

A full minute passed.

Unknown Number: Soon.

The screen went dark.

Emily lay back against her pillow, heart thudding—not from panic, but from the unsettling sense that something had shifted without moving.

Not uncovered.

Not revealed.

Just acknowledged.

Down the hall, Kate murmured in her sleep, a half-formed laugh that faded as quickly as it came. The sound anchored Emily to the present, to the house and the life still unfolding around her.

She closed her eyes.

The lake wasn't calling.

It was waiting.

And somewhere beneath the waterline, something remained—not because it was hidden, but because once it was down there, no one had been able to bring themselves to reach for it again.

CHAPTER SEVEN

Loose Panels

Emily went back alone the next morning.

Not because she'd planned to. Not because she'd decided anything in the clear, deliberate way decisions were supposed to happen. She woke before her alarm, lay there listening to the house settle, and knew—without urgency, without argument—that staying home would feel like lying.

The morning was already warm. Not hot yet, but headed there. The kind of heat that pressed in quietly, settling into wood and fabric and skin before anyone thought to complain. Kate was still asleep down the hall. Her mom's door was closed. No one asked where Emily was going when she grabbed her keys.

Outside, the light felt wrong—too gentle for what she knew was waiting.

The road to the overlook was empty this early. No trucks parked crooked at the shoulder. No tourists stopping to read signs they wouldn't remember. Just pavement, dust, and the low hum of tires moving through air that hadn't been disturbed yet.

Emily slowed as she climbed, her foot easing off the gas without her quite deciding to. The fence came into view gradually, not dramatic, not looming. Just there. A line of metal stitched along the ridge like an afterthought.

In daylight, it looked different.

Less like a boundary. More like a suggestion someone had meant to return to and never quite did.

She parked farther back than usual and walked the rest of the way, boots crunching softly over gravel. The sound carried more than she liked. Everything felt louder this morning—the wind brushing through grass, the faint clink of metal somewhere down the line, the hollow space where water used to be pulling sound downward instead of reflecting it back.

Emily stopped a few feet from the fence and pretended to read the warning sign bolted to one of the posts.

NO TRESPASSING
UNSTABLE GROUND
AUTHORIZED PERSONNEL ONLY

She knew the words by heart. She knew how recently the sign had been replaced—new screws, no rust yet. An update meant to reassure, not to stop anyone who had already decided.

Below her, Evansville lay open and pale, the basin exposed in a way that still didn't look real. The land hadn't changed shape so much as revealed it—seams and dips and darker stretches where water clung stubbornly to the lowest places. From this angle, the Jennings place was just another irregular shadow among many.

Almost.

Emily's gaze kept returning to it, drawn not by size but by refusal. The foundation didn't blend the way everything else did. It resisted the flattening effect of distance, its outline wrong in a way she couldn't have articulated if asked.

She stepped closer.

The fence shifted.

Not dramatically. Just enough to register. A soft metallic rattle that traveled a few panels down the line before settling again.

Emily frowned.

"That's not new," she murmured.

She walked along the fence, fingers hovering just short of contact, tracking the sound to its source. One panel leaned more than the others—not enough to be obvious unless you were looking for it. The post beside it had tilted slightly, the ground around its base fractured in a thin crescent where soil had pulled away.

She crouched, studying the bolt that held the panel in place.

It wasn't loose.

It was worse than that.

The threads were stripped, metal worn smooth by repeated tightening that no longer caught. Someone had been here recently. Someone had tried to make it hold.

Emily straightened slowly, her stomach tightening—not fear, not yet. Recognition.

A truck crunched to a stop behind her.

She didn't turn.

She didn't need to.

Blake's presence announced itself the way it always did—not loudly, not abruptly. Just a shift in the air, a change in how space arranged itself.

"You shouldn't be here," he said.

Not sharp. Not angry.

Just factual.

Emily turned. "Neither should that panel."

Blake followed her gaze immediately, eyes narrowing as he took in the lean, the fracture in the soil, the way the metal no longer quite trusted itself.

"That one again," he said. "I tightened it yesterday."

"And?" Emily asked.

He exhaled, rubbing the back of his neck. "And it didn't hold. The ground's moving more than they expected."

Emily nodded. "The bolt's stripped."

Blake looked at her sharply. "You sure?"

She crouched again, this time touching it—lightly, deliberately. The bolt turned without resistance, metal sliding uselessly against metal.

"It's not catching," she said. "You can tighten it, but it'll work itself loose. Especially if someone leans on it."

Blake swore under his breath—not angry. Tired.

He reached into his pocket and held out his Leatherman.

"Try it," he said. "Don't force it."

Emily took the tool. Their fingers brushed—brief, incidental, not intimate. She worked carefully, angling the bolt, applying pressure the way her dad had taught her fixing loose boards at home. Slow. Testing. Listening to the material instead of imposing will on it.

The metal protested.

Then—barely—settled.

"There," she said, straightening. "It'll hold longer. But not forever."

Blake took the tool back, watching the fence like it might answer him if he stared long enough.

"Thanks," he said.

Not casually. Not guarded.

Just honest.

They stood there for a moment, neither moving away.

The fence stretched on either side of them, uneven now that Emily was looking closely. Small inconsistencies—panels that leaned a fraction more, posts that no longer stood perfectly upright. It wasn't failure yet. But it was headed there.

"You don't have to keep doing this alone," Emily said.

Blake didn't answer right away.

He leaned against the fence beside her, forearms resting on the top rail, careful not to put his weight where it would matter. His gaze drifted toward the basin, settling where the ground darkened near the old foundation.

"My grandpa used to say fences aren't for keeping people out," he said finally. "They're for showing where someone stopped trying."

Emily swallowed.

"That doesn't make you responsible for it," she said.

Blake's mouth curved slightly. "Tell that to the town."

The wind moved through the grass below them, a low, restless sound. Somewhere farther down the fence line, metal clanged as another panel shifted—someone else adjusting, compensating, buying time.

Emily felt the odd tension of standing in a place that was both watched and neglected. Maintained, but only just enough. Controlled, but only on paper.

Blake shifted his weight, just enough that his shoulder brushed hers.

He didn't move away.

"You okay?" he asked, quieter now.

Emily nodded. "Yeah."

It wasn't the whole truth.

But it was enough for today.

They stood there longer than necessary, watching the basin the way people watched weather they couldn't change—alert, restrained, waiting for signs they'd recognize too late.

Below them, the valley stayed still.

Unchanged.

Unbothered by the line drawn above it.

Emily felt something settle in her chest—not relief, not resolve. Just the strange steadiness of not being alone at the edge anymore.

Not because someone had fixed the problem.

But because someone else had seen it fail.

And stayed anyway.

CHAPTER EIGHT

What Doesn't Move

The town reacted the way it always did—by pretending nothing had happened.

Emily noticed it in the pauses. Conversations that stopped when she stepped into the hardware store. The way people checked the fence line from their trucks but didn't slow down. The new flyers taped to the bulletin board outside the café, already curling at the corners:

HISTORICAL SOCIETY REMINDER
NO TRESPASSING
AREA UNDER REVIEW

Under review sounded temporary. Like attention would pass.

Emily doubted it.

She drove home instead of heading anywhere else, taking the longer way through side streets where the shade lingered longer, and the houses sat closer together, their porches facing one another like they shared secrets. Wind chimes clinked softly. Somewhere, a dog barked and then went quiet.

Her phone stayed still in the cup holder.

She didn't check it.

* * *

Martha was already at the kitchen table when Emily came in, shelling peas into a bowl that was nearly full, another waiting beside it. The radio played low—classic country, the kind that didn't ask for much.

"You're quiet," Martha said without looking up.

"I don't feel like talking," Emily said.

"That's allowed," Martha replied easily. "Sit anyway."

Emily took the chair across from her. The table was worn smooth in places, the wood lighter where hands had rested for years. Martha pushed the second bowl toward her.

"Help," she said. Not a request. Not a command. An invitation.

Emily took a pod and split it open, letting the peas drop.

They worked in silence for a few minutes.

Then Martha said, "The fence rattled all night."

Emily's fingers stilled.

"I heard it from the guest room," Martha continued. "Wind, mostly. But not only wind."

Emily swallowed. "Did you... call someone?"

"No," Martha said. "I figured if they wanted to hear it, they would."

Emily studied her grandmother's face—calm, focused, unreadable in the way of someone who'd learned which questions not to ask out loud.

"People are saying things," Emily said carefully.

Martha nodded once. "They always do."

"About Clara."

The peas clicked softly against the bowl.

Martha's hands didn't stop moving, but her shoulders tightened just enough for Emily to notice.

"She was my best friend," Martha said. Not defensive. Not fragile. Just factual.

"I know."

"Do you?" Martha asked, finally lifting her eyes. "Or do you know the version people settled on?"

Emily didn't answer.

Martha looked back down. "Grief makes people tidy. They want a story they can live with."

Emily felt the weight of that settle between them.

"Tom doesn't know everything," Martha added. "He knows what he was there for."

"And you?" Emily asked quietly.

Martha's fingers paused. Just for a second.

"I know what I carried home," she said. "And what I couldn't."

Emily nodded. It wasn't an answer. But it wasn't nothing.

* * *

That night, Emily stood at her bedroom window and watched the trees shift in the breeze. The hills cut a dark line against the sky, the basin hidden beyond them, out of sight but not out of mind.

Her phone buzzed.

She didn't jump this time.

Unknown Number: They're going to move the fence again.

Emily exhaled slowly.

Emily: Why?

The reply came faster than she expected.

Unknown Number: Because someone complained. Because it's easier to shift metal than memory.

Emily stared at the words.

Emily: Are you trying to help me?

Three dots appeared.

Disappeared.

Reappeared.

Unknown Number: I'm trying to keep this from choosing you.

Emily's throat tightened.

Emily: I didn't ask for this.

A pause.

Unknown Number: Neither did she.

The screen went dark.

* * *

On her way down the hall, Emily noticed Kate's sketchbook open on the floor again, the same drawing darkened almost to the point of tearing the page.

Emily lay back on her bed, staring at the ceiling fan as it turned slow and uneven, the rhythm just off enough to notice.

The fence.

The door.

The letters.

All of it rearranging itself without actually moving.

Outside, something shifted—branches scraping, gravel crunching faintly on the road. Emily held her breath until the sound passed, leaving only the steady hum of night.

The town wasn't haunted.

It was weighted.

And Emily was beginning to understand that some things didn't need to surface to pull you under.

They just needed you to stand too close for too long.

CHAPTER NINE

What Was Printed

The library smelled like dust and summer—old paper, sun-warmed carpet, and something faintly lemony from a cleaner that never quite erased the past.

Emily hadn't been inside it in years. Not since middle school, when research meant printing Wikipedia articles and calling it a day. Back then, the building had felt bigger somehow—endless shelves, the promise of answers if you were willing to look hard enough. Now it felt smaller, quieter. Like it had learned how to hold its breath.

Light slanted through the tall front windows, stopping short of the deepest shelves. Fans turned lazily overhead, pushing warm air from one corner to another without ever quite cooling it. Somewhere near the circulation desk, a printer hummed and then fell silent again.

Zoe dropped into a chair across from Emily at one of the long tables, sunglasses shoved up into her hair, foot hooked around the rung like she planned to bolt at any second.

"Okay," Zoe said. "We're officially being weird in public now."

Emily slid the first yearbook across the table. The cover was faded blue, the lettering cracked at the corners where it had been handled too often and then not at all.

Evansville High School — Class of 1965.

"This is normal," Emily said. "People do research all the time."

"People also Google things," Zoe replied. "Not dig through forty-year-old books like they're summoning something."

Emily ignored her and opened the cover.

The pages smelled different inside—mustier, older, like they'd been closed too long. The paper was thick and slightly rough under her fingers, the ink pressed deep enough that you could feel it if you traced the letters. Names marched in neat columns. Club photos. Sports teams. Smiling administrators in stiff poses.

A town arranged the way it wanted to remember itself.

Blake joined them a moment later, setting a stack of microfilm boxes on the table with more care than necessary. They made a soft, hollow sound as they landed, plastic against wood.

"Mrs. Henley says these are the last of the local papers before consolidation," he said. "After that, everything went county-wide."

Emily looked up. "She just... gave them to you?"

Blake shrugged. "I volunteer. It helps."

Emily thought about how much *help* could mean when you were tall, broad-shouldered, and generally left alone by people who assumed you belonged wherever you stood.

Zoe raised an eyebrow. "Since when do you volunteer for anything that doesn't involve manual labor or avoiding people?"

Blake shot her a look. "Since today."

Emily hid a smile and turned the page.

Graduation photos came first.

Rows of caps midair. Faces tilted up. Sunlight caught in fabric and hair and expressions that hadn't yet learned how to guard themselves. The moment was frozen mid-celebration—motion implied, joy suspended.

Emily's fingers slowed.

"There," she said.

Zoe leaned in. Blake stepped closer, one hand braced on the table.

Clara Jennings stood near the center of the photo, gown light against the darker shapes around her. Her cap was already off, hair loose and wind-touched, her face turned slightly toward someone just out of frame.

She was smiling.

Not politely. Not nervously.

Like someone who had already chosen where she was going next.

Zoe studied the image for a long moment, head tilted.

"That doesn't look like someone halfway out the door," she said.

Emily shook her head. "No. That looks like someone who expected to come back."

The words settled between them, heavier for having been spoken aloud.

Blake didn't say anything. His gaze stayed on the photo, jaw tight—not guarded, but focused. Like he was recalibrating something he'd been carrying for a long time without ever naming it.

Emily turned the page.

Clara appeared again—debate club, drama cast, swim team, a candid shot labeled *Senior Picnic*. In every one, she looked comfortable in her body, present. Leaning in. Laughing. Mid-gesture. Rooted in the frame even when she was caught in motion.

Emily's attention snagged on other faces as she turned the pages—her grandparents, younger than she'd ever seen them, standing shoulder to shoulder with classmates she recognized only from stories.

A few pages later, she found Blake's grandfather too, caught mid-laugh in a candid shot that felt impossibly alive.

These weren't ghosts.

These were people who still lived here. Who still remembered.

Emily traced the caption beneath one photo with her fingertip.

"She's everywhere," she said quietly.

"And not disappearing," Zoe added.

"This isn't how people talk about her," Zoe said after a moment.

"No," Emily agreed. "It's how they edited her."

Blake slid one of the microfilm reels closer. "Try June," he said. "The week after graduation."

Emily moved to the machine, threading the reel carefully the way Mrs. Henley had shown her years ago. The motor whirred to life, the screen flickering as she scrolled.

Headlines blurred past.

DAM PROJECT MOVES AHEAD OF SCHEDULE
EVANSVILLE RESIDENTS PREPARE FOR FINAL WEEK
GRADUATION MARKS END OF ERA

The language was celebratory. Forward-looking. Careful not to linger.

Then—

LOCAL GIRL REPORTED MISSING AFTER CEREMONY

Emily stopped.

The article was short. Precise in its vagueness. Full of words like *uncertain* and *unconfirmed*. It mentioned celebration. Confusion. Water rising in stages. It did not mention searching the shoreline. It did not mention where Clara was last seen. It did not mention who last spoke to her.

Halfway down, in a paragraph that felt more like a formality than a plea, was the only detail that anchored her to a life outside the headline.

The article identified her as Clara Jennings, only child of Edmond and Elizabeth Jennings, longtime Evansville residents.

Emily stared at the line longer than the rest.

"No siblings," she said quietly.

Zoe frowned, leaning closer as if proximity could change what was printed. "And if her parents are gone..."

"Then the search would've ended with them," Emily finished.

A silence followed that felt different than the others—less about what they didn't know, more about what the town had been willing to let fade.

"It just... stops," Zoe said, voice lower now.

"That's how they wanted it," Blake replied. "Nothing to investigate if nothing's specific."

Emily leaned back, pulse steady but heavy.

"They didn't know," she said slowly. "Or they decided knowing would be worse."

No one argued.

Emily closed the yearbook gently, as if sound alone might disturb what they'd uncovered.

Outside, a truck passed, gravel crunching on pavement. Someone laughed near the front desk. Life moving forward, as it always did.

But something had shifted.

Not because they'd found anything new.

Because the story they'd been given no longer fit what had been printed in ink and light and faces that hadn't yet learned how to disappear.

The record hadn't lied.

It had simply been allowed to speak without being heard.

Emily felt a quiet resolve settle in her chest—not urgency, not fear. Just certainty.

She was done accepting the tidy version.

Somewhere beneath the waterline, the truth hadn't moved.

It had just been waiting for someone to recognize it.

CHAPTER TEN

Contour Lines

The historical society didn't call it a meeting.

They called it an *update*, like information could be delivered without changing the shape of a room.

Emily saw the flyer taped to the café window on her way back to her truck—white paper, black block letters, corners already curling in the heat.

HISTORICAL SOCIETY UPDATE
PINE VALLEY BASIN ACCESS & SAFETY
TONIGHT — 6:30 P.M.
COMMUNITY ROOM (BEHIND THE LIBRARY)

Below it, in smaller print:

PLEASE RESPECT BARRIERS
PLEASE REPORT TRESPASSING

Report made it sound small. Like a broken streetlight. Like something easily fixed.

Emily kept walking. The words followed anyway.

Her phone stayed silent.

That felt deliberate.

***

Zoe texted at three.

Zoe: you going tonight
Zoe: because i am

Zoe: and if you say no i'm not pretending i'm not mad

Emily stared at the screen, then typed.

Emily: I'm going.

Zoe: good

Zoe: wear your "i belong here" face

Emily snorted despite herself.

* * *

Kate was sprawled on the living room floor, completely absorbed in something she'd spread out across an old towel.

Charcoal smudged her fingers. A sketchbook lay open beside her, pages weighted down with a smooth gray rock she'd brought in from outside. She was working the same shape over and over — a rectangle, drawn lightly, erased, then redrawn darker.

It wasn't a door exactly. Just the suggestion of one.

"You're going somewhere," Kate said without looking up.

Emily paused. "What makes you say that?"

"You changed out of lake clothes," Kate replied. "And you didn't grab snacks. That means serious."

Emily glanced down. Jeans. Real ones.

"It's a meeting," she said.

Kate finally looked up. Her hands froze mid-stroke. "The lake one?"

Emily hesitated. "Yes."

Kate studied her face longer than necessary, then looked back down at her drawing. She darkened a line, then another.

"Are they going to say anything real?" she asked.

Emily didn't answer fast enough.

Kate exhaled through her nose. "They never do."

Emily crouched beside her, lowering her voice. "I'll be back later."

Kate nodded once. "Okay."

It wasn't relief. It was trust.

Emily hated that she might break it.

***

The community room smelled like folding chairs and dust and the faint lemon of old cleaner.

People filtered in quietly. Not the whole town—just enough. Enough to feel watched without knowing by whom.

Emily took a seat near the front. Zoe slid in beside her, knee bouncing.

"Look at us," Zoe murmured. "Participating."

Emily didn't smile.

Blake came in through the side door, already carrying a stack of chairs like he'd been assigned the task before he arrived. He didn't look at Emily right away.

Then he did.

A flicker of recognition. A pause.

Then back to work.

Zoe noticed. Of course she did.

"Oh," she whispered. "That's a look."

Emily kept her eyes forward. "Don't."

Mrs. Henley stepped up to the microphone and tapped it once. The squeal made everyone flinch, then settle.

"Thank you for coming," she said, voice warm and practiced. "We'll keep this brief."

A ripple moved through the room. People didn't trust brief.

"The dam maintenance is proceeding as planned," Mrs. Henley said. "The drawdown is temporary. The basin will refill once repairs are complete."

Emily's jaw tightened.

"As a result of increased foot traffic," Mrs. Henley continued, "the county has designated the basin a restricted area due to unstable ground."

She didn't say *because people are curious*. She didn't say *because something was found*.

"Additional fencing will be installed," Mrs. Henley said. "Panels will be reinforced. Access points reduced."

Someone muttered, "So they're sealing it."

Mrs. Henley smiled tightly. "They're making it safe."

A man raised his hand. "Are there cameras?"

Another voice answered without waiting. "They don't need cameras if people report what they see."

That landed harder.

A woman near the aisle stood. "What about Clara Jennings?"

The room went still—not shocked, just alert.

Mrs. Henley didn't hesitate. "Clara Jennings' disappearance was investigated at the time."

"That's not what I asked," the woman said. "Are you going to acknowledge her as part of what's down there?"

Mrs. Henley inhaled slowly. "We are not reopening that case."

A low murmur followed. Not anger—calculation.

Zoe leaned toward Emily. "That was the line."

Emily nodded.

"The historical society will be documenting visible structures and cataloging artifacts," Mrs. Henley continued. "We ask that anyone with photographs, letters, or documents related to Evansville contact us so they can be preserved appropriately."

Collected, Emily thought.

Curated.

Controlled.

"That's all for tonight," Mrs. Henley said. "Thank you for caring about our shared history."

Chairs scraped. Voices rose. Small groups formed like weather systems.

Emily stood.

Blake was already folding chairs again, moving fast. When she approached, he didn't look up.

"You shouldn't have come," he said quietly.

Emily blinked. "You say that like I had a choice."

"People noticed," he replied.

Zoe crossed her arms. "People always notice."

"Not like this," Blake said.

Emily lowered her voice. "They're reinforcing tomorrow."

Blake nodded. "Early."

Zoe's eyes widened. "So that's it."

Blake glanced toward the doorway. "You need to leave."

Emily felt the vibration before she reached her phone.

Unknown Number: They're tightening lines where the ground won't hold.

Blake saw her face change.

"Did you show anyone those messages?" he asked.

Emily shook her head.

"Good," he said. Then, quieter: "Put it away."

She did.

Zoe grabbed Emily's arm. "We're going."

They stepped outside into warm air and pine and the relief of space.

Halfway to the cars, Blake caught up.

"Tomorrow morning," he said. "Not tonight."

Zoe scoffed. "Because daylight makes crimes better?"

"Because they expect night," Blake replied. "Fear works better in the dark."

Emily met his eyes. "I just need to see it again."

Blake held her gaze. "You can't go alone."

"I wasn't planning to."

Zoe stared between them. "I hate both of you."

Blake's mouth curved slightly. "Tomorrow. Early. Then you stop."

Emily didn't argue. Not because she agreed.

Because she knew he was trying to hold a line that was already eroding.

Zoe unlocked her car. "Fine. But if this goes badly, I get to say I told you so forever."

Emily almost smiled.

Almost.

She got into her truck, phone face-down in the cup holder.

The library lights glowed behind her, calm and harmless.

The basin waited.

And the line the town had drawn suddenly felt very thin—not because it could be crossed, but because it had been drawn too late.

CHAPTER ELEVEN

Sightlines

They parked farther down the road than they had the night before—not out of caution, just habit. Morning had a way of flattening things, making yesterday's urgency feel premature.

The fence line was quiet.

No workers. No trucks. No sense of interruption. Just metal panels stitched along the basin's edge, pale and still in the early light.

Zoe shaded her eyes. "Looks... normal."

Blake nodded. "It is."

That mattered. Emily hadn't realized how much she'd been bracing for something else—voices, questions, attention. But the town hadn't noticed them. Hadn't marked them. There was no proof of anything to notice.

They walked the fence line slowly. Not searching—just moving, like three people with nowhere else they needed to be.

From the slight rise near the overlook, the basin opened below them. In daylight, the valley looked less ominous than it had at night, more legible. The foundations were laid out clearly in the morning light, lines and shapes pressed into the mud like a map that refused to fold away.

Emily stopped.

From here, the Jennings place was visible—downslope, set apart by the darker water pooled beside it. The shallow basin beside the foundation hadn't changed. The water was still. Reflective. Almost ordinary.

Almost.

Emily crouched near the fence rail, careful not to lean too far forward. From this distance, she could see the straight edge beneath the surface—the metal frame that cut too clean a line through water that should've softened everything.

Blake followed her gaze. "You're seeing it from here?"

"Yes."

He didn't question it. Just nodded, once.

Zoe shifted her weight. "So we're clear—this is still outside the fence. We are aggressively not trespassing."

Emily exhaled softly. "Yes."

"Good," Zoe said. "Because I don't feel like explaining anything to anyone ever."

They stood there in silence.

No sounds rose from the basin. No movement. Just the faint rustle of grass behind them and the dry click of fence panels cooling in the sun.

"They didn't move anything," Zoe said finally.

"No," Blake agreed. "They adjusted posts. Tightened where it sagged."

Emily frowned. "That's it?"

"That's it."

No drama. No sweep. No sealing-off moment. Just maintenance.

Emily straightened, brushing dust from her knees. "So if someone wanted to see it—really see it—they still could."

Blake's jaw tightened. "From here. Yes."

Zoe glanced between them. "And that's the part that doesn't sit right."

Emily didn't argue.

Her phone buzzed once in her pocket—not a text. Just a notification. Weather. Nothing that mattered.

They walked back along the fence without speaking, the Jennings place slipping out of view as the ground leveled again. When they reached the truck, Blake paused.

"This doesn't mean anything yet," he said.

Emily nodded. "I know."

"But it's enough to keep noticing," Zoe added.

Emily met her eyes. "Yes."

They drove away without looking back.

The basin remained exactly as it was—open, quiet, unclaimed. Nothing disturbed. Nothing resolved.

Just a place waiting for someone to come closer.

CHAPTER TWELVE

Angles of Light

The overlook felt different in the morning.

Not quieter—there was wind, distant traffic, the scrape of boots somewhere behind them—but thinner, like the space itself had lost some of its patience. Emily rested her forearms on the railing without leaning, the metal already warm beneath her skin.

Below them, the basin lay open and colorless, a shallow bowl of geometry and dust. Foundations cut pale shapes into the earth. Pools of remaining water caught the sky in broken strips.

Nothing looked hidden.

That was the problem.

Zoe squinted against the sun. "So this is it," she said. "This is what everyone's pretending is fine."

Blake didn't answer. He was watching the fence line farther down, where new panels had been stacked but not yet installed. Nothing moved there. No one was working yet.

Emily lifted the binoculars and brought them to her eyes.

From above, Evansville looked flatter than she expected. Less like a place and more like a diagram. Streets reduced to faint scars. Buildings to outlines that only held if you already knew what they were.

She swept slowly.

Whitman's Grocery.

The barbershop.

The Grange Hall.

Then the Jennings place.

Emily paused.

The pool beside the foundation was darker than the rest. Not deeper—she could see the bottom in places—but less responsive to the light. Where other puddles reflected the sky in bright fragments, this one stayed flat, dull, absorbing more than it returned.

She adjusted the focus.

The shape didn't sharpen.

It fractured instead—shadow bending where it shouldn't, edges slipping as soon as she tried to follow them. The longer she looked, the less coherent it became.

Emily lowered the binoculars.

Zoe noticed immediately. "What?"

"I don't know," Emily said. Then, after a beat, "It's not behaving like the rest."

Zoe took the binoculars. She leaned forward, braced herself, adjusted the wheel with exaggerated care.

Her mouth tightened.

"That's... not a thing," she said.

Blake glanced at her. "Define not a thing."

Zoe handed the binoculars back. "It won't resolve. It's like—" She made a vague gesture with her hand. "Like it's refusing to be one shape."

Emily lifted the camera and framed the same area. She snapped a photo, then checked the screen.

The image looked ordinary.

Flat. Distant. The darker patch barely registered, just another uneven shadow in a basin full of them.

Zoe peered over her shoulder. "That's nothing."

Emily nodded. "Exactly."

Blake exhaled slowly. "If it were structural, someone would've logged it already."

"I know," Emily said.

She didn't argue. She didn't insist.

She just kept watching.

The wind shifted. Light slid across the basin, changing angles, changing contrast. For a moment, the darker patch seemed to deepen. Then it vanished into sameness again.

Emily lowered the camera.

Zoe rocked back on her heels. "So what now?"

Emily didn't answer right away.

Below them, the Jennings foundation stayed where it was. Unremarkable. Unnamed. Doing nothing at all.

But Emily felt the same pressure she had for days now—not fear, not urgency. Just insistence. The sense of something holding its position while everything else adjusted around it.

"We don't do anything from here," she said finally.

Zoe blinked. "That's... surprisingly mature."

Emily didn't smile. "Because this doesn't tell us anything yet."

Blake nodded once. "Good."

They stood there a moment longer, the three of them watching the basin settle into its midday glare.

Nothing surfaced.

Nothing shifted.

Nothing asked to be seen.

But as they turned away, Emily knew one thing with absolute clarity:

Whatever was down there wasn't meant to be found from a distance.

It required proximity.

And when the time came—when the angle was no longer wrong—she would be close enough to know the difference.

CHAPTER THIRTEEN

Pressure Points

Blake picked Emily up first.

She climbed into the truck without a word, the vinyl bench already warm from the early sun. The smell inside was dust and old fabric, faintly gasoline, like the cab had absorbed a hundred summer days and never quite let them go. Blake waited while she slid across toward the driver's side, then shut her door and pulled away from the curb. The engine's low vibration settled into her bones.

They didn't talk.

Emily watched his hands on the wheel—steady, relaxed in a way that didn't match the tightness in his jaw. He drove like he'd done this route so many times his body could do it without his mind, but today every movement felt deliberate, controlled. As if he were keeping his grip on more than the truck.

Zoe was waiting when they reached her place, backpack slung over one shoulder. She climbed in last, settling into the passenger side and tugging her hoodie sleeves down over her hands as Blake put the truck back in gear.

No one commented on the seating.

No one joked.

Emily felt it anyway—the unspoken arrangement. Zoe up front to watch. Emily closer to Blake not because of comfort, but because if something happened, he could reach her without having to think. It was the kind of logic people used in emergencies, the kind they pretended wasn't happening by never naming it out loud.

The road toward Pine Valley was quiet. Morning light flattened the landscape, washing color out of the hills. Dust lifted behind them as pavement gave way to gravel, the tires singing softly against stone.

Zoe broke the silence first. "So we're clear on the plan."

Blake kept his eyes on the road. "We park at the service pullout. We walk in together. We don't split up."

"And we don't improvise," Zoe said.

Emily swallowed. "We're just confirming."

Blake's jaw tightened. "Yes."

The word felt like a boundary, not reassurance.

* * *

They parked once.

The service pullout was nothing more than a widened shoulder where county trucks sometimes idled. No signage. No markers. Just scrub grass bent flat by tires and a view down toward the basin that looked deceptively calm.

The fence line waited downslope, dull metal catching what little light there was. From here, the Jennings place wasn't visible—only distance and shape, the pale bowl of earth like something scooped out and left exposed.

"That's good," Zoe muttered. "Means we're not obvious."

Blake shut off the engine and sat for a beat, listening. Emily realized he was waiting for something—voices, footsteps, the clink of tools. Proof they weren't alone.

Nothing.

He nodded once, like he'd been given permission.

Blake led them along the fence, keeping low, until they reached a shallow dip where erosion had lifted the bottom edge just enough to slip through without rattling the posts. He held the panel steady as Zoe went first, then Emily, then eased himself through last, careful not to let the metal sing.

On the other side, the basin opened up.

They moved carefully after that, following firmer ground Blake knew by instinct now—old poured sections, compacted earth where foundations once met. No sidewalks. No paths. Just judgment.

The basin smelled like dry mud and iron, like sun-baked clay that still remembered water. Heat was already rising off the ground, but the light was muted, pale, as if the day hadn't fully decided to arrive yet.

Emily felt the shift before she saw it: the way sound thinned, the way the air seemed to settle differently as they approached the Jennings foundation. It wasn't fear exactly. It was something older. Like walking into a room where an argument had happened and ended before you arrived.

The shallow pool beside the foundation lay unnaturally still, its surface clear enough to see straight down. No wind disturbed it. No insect touched it. It didn't ripple the way water should.

The cellar door did not announce itself.

It only appeared once you were close enough to kneel.

Blake crouched first, brushing silt aside. The metal frame emerged slowly, deliberate, its edges intact where everything else had softened with time. Rust rimmed the hinges, but the shape held.

Zoe sucked in a breath. "Okay. That's not nothing."

Emily dropped beside Blake. Up close, the water was impossibly clear. The door sat beneath it, sealed, weighted, hinges rusted but holding.

"This is why they missed it," Blake said quietly. "You can't see it unless you're already here."

Emily nodded. Her pulse felt steady. Too steady.

Blake shifted his weight, planting one knee, testing the frame with his fingers. "I can't do this alone," he said.

"I know," Emily replied.

For a moment, all three of them hovered at the edge of action—the last second before something crossed a line that couldn't be uncrossed. Zoe met Emily's eyes and gave a single nod.

They lifted together.

The seal broke with a low, reluctant sound, and water slid aside just enough for what lay beneath to become visible.

Emily saw it first—not because she was looking harder, but because she couldn't look away.

Bone.

A pale curve held in impossible clarity beneath the water, unmistakable once your eye knew what it was meant to see. And above it—fine fracture lines where the shape should have been smooth.

Zoe's breath left her in a single, broken sound.

"Oh," she said quietly.

Then, softer—like saying it too loud might make it real—

"...the skull."

The word landed.

Emily's vision tunneled. The basin tilted. The sky swam above her—pale, distant, the edges of her vision threaded with black. Her knees folded without warning.

Blake caught her before she hit the ground.

* * *

She came back in pieces.

Sound first—muted, distorted. Then weight: her cheek pressed into Blake's shoulder, her fingers twisted in the fabric of his shirt. His heartbeat was steady beneath her ear.

"I've got you," he said, low and unwavering. "I've got you."

Zoe hovered close, face pale but controlled. "We're leaving. Now."

Blake didn't argue. He lifted Emily fully, her weight slack against him, and turned away from the foundation without looking back. Zoe moved ahead, checking footing, clearing the path.

They didn't run.

They didn't speak.

At the fence line, Blake stopped long enough to assess the gap they'd used going in. He eased Emily down just enough to guide her through first, one hand steady at her back, then followed, careful to keep the panel from rattling as Zoe slipped through after them.

Only once they were clear did he let himself exhale.

At the pullout, Blake set Emily down against the side of the truck, keeping an arm around her shoulders until the ground steadied beneath her feet.

Zoe opened the passenger door. "River," she said.

Blake nodded.

Emily didn't protest as they loaded back in—Emily first, sliding across the bench; Zoe climbing in after her. Blake took the wheel, hands firm, knuckles pale until the road leveled.

The basin disappeared behind them.

* * *

They stopped where the river widened and slowed, water moving fast enough to carry sound away.

Emily sat on a flat rock at the edge, shoes pulled off, feet submerged in the cold current. The shock grounded her where the basin had hollowed her out. The water pressed against her ankles, constant, undeniable.

"She didn't drown," Zoe said quietly.

Emily nodded. "No."

Blake stared at the current. "She was already gone."

No one added more.

Emily pressed her palms to her thighs, breathing until the shaking eased. "We don't touch anything again."

Blake nodded. "We tip the county. Anonymous."

"And we step back," Zoe said. "No names. No stories."

Emily closed her eyes once. "Yes."

The river kept moving.

Behind them, the basin remained exactly as it had been—quiet, unchanged, no longer able to keep what it held.

And for the first time since the water had receded, Emily knew with certainty:

The truth wasn't hidden anymore.

It was simply waiting to be acknowledged.

CHAPTER FOURTEEN

Aftermath Logistics

The drive back from the river was quiet in the way a room gets quiet after something breaks.

Not the fragile quiet of anticipation. The aftermath quiet. The kind that arrives once there's nothing left to argue about.

The pickup smelled like sun-warmed vinyl and wet stone. Wind threaded through the cracked window and dried the damp along Emily's wrists where she'd rinsed her hands without really thinking. She could still feel the cold of the river there, pressed into her skin like a memory that hadn't decided whether to fade or bruise.

Zoe sat rigid by the passenger door, staring out like she could keep the world in place by watching it. Her knee bounced once, then stilled. Control regained by force.

Emily sat in the middle, knees turned slightly toward Blake because there wasn't anywhere else for them to go.

Blake drove with both hands on the wheel.

Not tense.

Not frantic.

Just fixed.

Emily watched the knuckles whiten and then ease, whiten and then ease, like his body was doing math her brain couldn't solve yet. She wondered if he even noticed. She wondered if this was how he always handled pressure—by narrowing everything down to what still functioned.

No one spoke until Zoe cleared her throat.

"So," she said, voice careful. "We're doing the anonymous thing."

Blake didn't look at her. "Yes."

The word was final. Not dismissive. Settled.

Emily swallowed. Her tongue felt too big for her mouth. "We have to. If we don't—"

"If we don't," Zoe cut in, "we become the people who knew and didn't say anything."

That landed hard in the center of Emily's chest, like something finding its mark.

Blake's jaw worked once. "We don't talk about it to anyone else. Not friends. Not parents. Not your grandpa. Nobody."

The word *grandpa* sat between them like a test. Emily nodded anyway, even though it already felt like lying, even if it wasn't. Even if silence, in this case, was the cost of doing it right.

They passed the turnoff to the reservoir without looking. The trees swallowed the view. The basin ceased to exist again—at least from the road.

Emily's phone vibrated once in her pocket.

Not a text.

Just a pulse of signal.

She didn't take it out. If she looked, she might expect something. She wasn't ready for that yet.

Blake spoke again, quieter. "We do it tonight."

Zoe finally glanced over, eyes sharp. "The email."

Blake nodded once.

Emily's throat tightened. "You're sure email is better than calling?"

"Calls get traced easier than you think," Blake said. "And if we say too much, they ask questions. We keep it simple. Location. What it is. That's it."

Zoe stared out the window again. "God, I hate being right about anything."

Emily let out a sound that wasn't a laugh. "Same."

Blake's gaze flicked to her—quick as a match strike—then back to the road.

He said nothing.

But his hand moved, just once, off the wheel long enough to touch her knee through the thin fabric of her jeans.

Not gripping. Not holding.

Just there.

A pressure point.

A reminder.

Emily's breath caught. She didn't look at him. If she looked at him, she might crack. Might say something she didn't have language for yet.

His hand returned to the wheel like it had never happened.

Zoe didn't notice.

Or pretended she didn't.

They drove on.

Zoe's place came first.

Blake slowed at the curb. Gravel popped under the tires. The engine dropped into a lower, steadier idle.

Zoe didn't move right away.

She turned halfway in her seat, looking at Emily like she was trying to memorize her exact shape. Like this might be the last version of her she got.

"Text me when you're inside," Zoe said.

Emily blinked. "I'm not getting out here."

"I know," Zoe said, impatient with her. "Text me anyway."

Emily nodded, because it was easier than arguing with the way Zoe's voice shook under the attitude.

Zoe opened the passenger door. The hinge squealed like it wanted attention. She stepped out, paused with one hand on the door frame, then leaned back in.

"And Emily," she said, lower now.

Emily met her eyes.

Zoe didn't say *be careful*.

Zoe didn't say *I told you so*.

She just said, "Don't do anything alone. Promise."

Emily's throat tightened. "I promise."

Zoe nodded once like she'd just gotten what she needed to keep breathing. Then she shut the door and walked up her steps without looking back.

Blake waited until Zoe was on the porch and inside before he pulled away.

Not because he was worried about Zoe.

Because it was the kind of person he was.

Emily watched Zoe's house disappear behind them.

Then the pickup filled with the sound of tires and wind and the quiet insistence of what they'd seen.

Emily's street came next. Familiar trees. Familiar mailboxes. Familiar porches.

Like nothing had happened.

Like everything had.

Blake parked in front of her house and killed the engine.

The silence that followed felt too complete.

Emily's hands were still in her lap. She hadn't realized she'd been holding them there like they belonged to someone else.

"Okay," Zoe had said earlier. Anonymous. Like that made it smaller.

Emily stared at her own front steps.

"You ready?" Blake asked.

His voice wasn't soft.

It was steady.

Emily nodded. "Yes."

But she didn't move.

Blake shifted slightly, turning just enough that his shoulder brushed hers. His hand found her again—this time not her knee, but her wrist. Two fingers on the inside, where her pulse kept insisting she was alive.

"You're shaking," he said.

"I'm not," Emily lied automatically.

Blake's mouth curved, barely. Not a smile. A recognition.

He didn't call her on it.

He just stayed where he was, fingers still on her wrist, until the shaking slowed enough to be less obvious.

Emily finally slid across the bench toward the passenger door.

Blake didn't move to help. Didn't crowd her. Didn't make it a thing.

He just watched her like he was making sure she remained real.

Emily opened the passenger door and stepped down. The ground felt too solid under her shoes, like the world was trying to pretend it had never been mud.

She shut the door and turned back.

Blake leaned across the bench to roll down the passenger window.

"Tonight," he said.

Emily nodded. "Tonight."

He hesitated, then added, "I can set it up—burner address, no names, no trace. But you decide what it says. And you press send."

That landed heavier than anything else had.

Zoe should know, Emily thought. Zoe had to know.

"She already knows," Blake said, like he'd heard her thoughts. "I told her. She hates it. Which means it's the right move."

Emily swallowed. "What are we saying?"

"Just facts," Blake said. "No names. No theories. No... anything that makes it personal."

Emily's chest tightened on the word *personal*.

Blake's gaze held hers through the open window.

Then his voice dipped—quiet enough that it didn't feel like a decision. Just a truth that had been waiting.

"I'm not leaving until you're inside."

Emily's breath caught.

She nodded once, like she could still operate her body.

She turned and walked up her steps.

Halfway to the porch, she stopped.

Not because she wanted drama.

Because she suddenly needed to look back.

Blake was still there, elbow on the wheel, watching her through the open passenger-side window like her outline mattered.

Emily didn't wave.

She just lifted her hand slightly—an acknowledgement without words.

Blake's throat moved like he swallowed something.

He didn't wave back.

He just stayed.

Emily went inside and shut the door behind her. The lock clicked too loudly in the quiet house.

Only then did she hear the truck start again.

Only then did she let herself breathe.

*　*　*

In her bedroom, Emily sat on the edge of her bed and stared at her phone until the screen dimmed.

Her hands smelled faintly of river water and metal.

Her brain kept replaying the moment the seal broke. The way the water moved aside. The way clarity had done what darkness couldn't.

Zoe's voice—small and broken—kept returning like a bruise you couldn't stop pressing.

Oh... the skull...

Emily's stomach rolled.

She stood and went to the bathroom, ran cold water, and held her wrists under it until the skin ached. It didn't help.

Nothing helped.

Down the hall, the house was quiet.

Her mom's voice drifted up from the kitchen—low, talking to Kate about something ordinary. Something safe.

Emily leaned her forehead against the bathroom door frame and tried not to cry, because crying felt like it would make it real in a way she wasn't ready for.

Her phone buzzed.

A text.

Zoe: you inside?

Emily stared at it for a long beat.

Emily: yes

Zoe: ok

Zoe: blake said you're doing it tonight

Emily: yeah

Zoe: em

Zoe: don't let your brain turn this into a dare

Emily's throat tightened.

Emily: i won't

Zoe: good

Zoe: because i need you alive

Emily stared at that last line until the letters blurred.

Then she set the phone face-down and pressed both palms to the sink.

Alive.

As if that was the baseline now.

* * *

That night, after the house had gone still, Emily sat in her dark room with her laptop open and the brightness turned low.

Blake's message came through first—short.

Blake: burner's ready. address is saved. no names. your call.

Emily's fingers hovered over the keys.

She reached back absently, tugging at the base of her braid until it loosened against her neck. A few strands slipped free and fell forward over her shoulder. She didn't fix them.

Her pulse thudded in her throat.

Emily: i'm going to do it now.

She kept it simple. Location. What they'd seen beneath the waterline. That it was sealed. That it needed a look—official, careful, immediate.

She read it twice. Once like a witness. Once like someone who could still choose.

Then she pressed **Send**.

Emily: sent.

Emily sat back against her pillows, staring at the ceiling fan as it turned slow and uneven.

Outside her window, the hills cut a dark line against the sky, and beyond them the basin waited where it always had.

Only now it wasn't just waiting.

Now it had been seen.

And somewhere in the dark, in an office with fluorescent lights and a file cabinet full of "closed" things, her email would land like a stone dropped into still water.

No name. No story.

Just the truth—small enough to be carried, heavy enough to sink.

Emily closed her eyes.

And for the first time since the water had receded, she understood something she hadn't wanted to know:

Finding her was only the beginning.

CHAPTER FIFTEEN

The Call Back

Emily woke to the sound of her mom moving around the kitchen like she was trying not to wake anyone.

Cabinets closed softly. The faucet ran in short bursts instead of one long rush. A spoon hit the counter once, then not again. The house wasn't quiet exactly—it was careful. The kind of careful that came from someone deciding, without saying it out loud, that today would require restraint.

Emily lay still, staring at the ceiling fan as it turned slow and uneven. The blades clicked faintly on one rotation, then didn't on the next. An inconsistency she couldn't stop tracking. She counted revolutions without meaning to. Lost track. Started again.

Last night hadn't ended.
It had only stopped talking.

She flexed her hands under the blanket. Her wrists ached in a dull, distant way, like a memory her body was holding onto even if her mind tried not to. If she focused too hard, she could still feel the river—cold, fast, indiscriminate. The way it hadn't cared what it carried. The way it hadn't slowed when it took something in.

Emily reached for her phone on the nightstand and flipped it over.

No new messages.

No unknown number.

Nothing from Zoe.

Nothing from Blake.

Just the time. 7:12.

Too early for anything official. Too late to pretend nothing had started.

She sat up slowly, waiting for the room to tilt. It didn't. That almost felt worse. Her mouth tasted faintly metallic, like she'd bitten the inside of her cheek sometime during the night and forgotten.

Down the hall, Kate's door was cracked open. Emily paused there longer than she meant to, listening to her sister's sleep—soft, untroubled, the kind that belonged to someone who didn't know the shape of a sealed door under water. The kind that trusted the world to stay arranged the way it had been when she closed her eyes.

Emily left Kate's door as it was and went downstairs.

Her mom was at the counter with a mug of coffee, hair clipped back, phone facedown beside a grocery list. The radio played low—nothing urgent, nothing new. A familiar morning voice murmured about weather and local events like the world hadn't been asked to adjust its tone.

"Morning," her mom said, looking up.

"Morning," Emily answered.

Her voice sounded normal. That almost made it worse.

Her mom studied her for a second, like she wanted to ask something and couldn't find a version that wouldn't start a fight or open something she wasn't ready to see. Emily felt the moment stretch, held between them by nothing but habit.

"Eggs are still warm," her mom said instead.

Emily took a plate and sat at the table. She stared at the eggs like they were a dare. Steam rose faintly, then disappeared. She cut into one, watched the yolk spread, then stopped. Appetite felt like a foreign concept—something she'd misplaced and would have to go back for later.

Kate drifted in a minute later in an oversized sweatshirt, eyes half open. She poured cereal, leaned on the counter, and then paused.

"You look tired," Kate said.

Emily's throat tightened. "Didn't sleep great."

Kate squinted like she didn't buy it, but she didn't press. Not yet. She took her bowl to the table and ate with exaggerated focus, as if silence itself might ask questions if she didn't keep moving.

Emily lifted her fork, set it down again. Her appetite had gone somewhere else entirely.

Her mom's phone vibrated on the counter.

Emily's eyes snapped to it.

Her mom glanced down, frowned, then ignored it. The screen went dark again.

Emily felt something settle in her chest—not fear exactly. Recognition. The sense that things were already moving without her permission. That the email had not gone unnoticed. That someone, somewhere, had read it and decided what came next.

Her phone buzzed in her pocket.

A call.

Unknown number.

Emily stood so fast her chair legs scraped the floor.

"Bathroom," she said quickly.

Her mom frowned. "Emily—"

"I'll be right back," Emily said, already moving.

She shut herself into the bathroom and locked the door before answering on the second ring.

"Hello?"

A man's voice, calm in the way people sound when they're trained not to panic. Not rushed. Not apologetic. Professional.

"Is this Emily Warren?"

Emily's grip tightened around the phone.

"Yes."

"This is Deputy Keller with Beaverhead County Sheriff's Office."

The words landed without drama. That was almost the worst part. No warning tone. No apology for the interruption. Just fact, delivered cleanly.

Emily stared at the tile floor, tracing a crack she'd memorized sometime in childhood. It ran from the baseboard toward the drain, splitting once, then disappearing beneath the cabinet.

"Okay," she managed.

"We received an anonymous report overnight about Pine Valley Reservoir," Keller said. "Possible human remains in the basin. I'm calling because the information included a landmark name—Jennings—and the historical society suggested you might recognize the area."

The name landed differently this time. Not like a story. Not like a rumor passed too many times to hold shape.

Like a coordinate.

Emily's stomach turned.

"Henley gave you my number?" she asked.

"She confirmed you've been asking about Evansville," Keller said, tone still even. "That's all. I'm not accusing you of anything. I'm trying to verify location before we send people into unstable ground."

Unstable.

Verify.

Possible.

Emily noticed the words because she needed something to hold onto besides the image rising uninvited behind her eyes. Bone. Water. The way clarity had been worse than darkness.

Emily pressed her free hand flat to the sink. The porcelain felt too cool. Too clean.

"I don't know who reported it," Emily said.

That was true. Even if she knew where the words had come from. Even if she could still feel the weight of pressing send.

Keller didn't push. "Understood. Do you know the Jennings foundation? Is there a pooled section of water there?"

Emily closed her eyes.

Her mind tried, uselessly, to soften the image—to blur it, distort it, turn it back into suggestion. But the clarity was fixed now. Bone. Water. The shape that refused to be anything else once it had named itself.

She could keep everything locked inside and still answer like a person with working eyes.

"Yes," she said carefully. "There's a darker pool by that foundation."

"Can you tell me the best access point?" Keller asked. "Where people have been getting in, even with the fence?"

Emily's throat tightened.

She pictured the loose panel. The bolt. The way they'd slid through like they belonged there. Like the fence was a suggestion, not a boundary. Like permission was something you took when no one was watching.

"I don't know about best," Emily said. "But people go down from the picnic shelter and the overlook. They find a way."

Keller made a soft sound—acknowledgment, not judgment.

"Okay," he said. "We're heading out. I'm going to ask you not to go back down there."

"I wasn't planning to," Emily said, and meant it.

There was a beat of silence. Not empty. Weighted.

Then Keller's voice shifted slightly—less procedural, more human.

"If anyone contacts you—press, neighbors, whoever—don't speculate," he said. "Let us confirm what's there first."

Emily swallowed. "People won't wait."

"I know," Keller said simply. "But you can."

Emily stared at her reflection in the mirror. She looked the same. Same hair pulled back too quickly. Same eyes that hadn't slept enough. That felt like a lie.

"I'm going to text you this number from a department line," Keller continued. "If you remember anything that helps us locate it safely, you can reply."

"Okay," Emily whispered.

He hung up.

A second later, a text arrived.

Deputy Keller (BCSO): This is Deputy Keller. Please don't go to the basin. If you recall additional details that help locate the area safely, you can reach me here.

Emily stared at the message until the words turned into shapes.

Then she set the phone down on the counter and bent forward, hands braced on the sink as her body caught up all at once. Nausea rolled through her, sharp and insistent. Her hands shook—not violently, but persistently. Like her body was reminding her it hadn't agreed to this pace.

She breathed until the edge dulled. Until the room stopped narrowing.

She rehearsed what she would say downstairs. Once. Twice. Each version sounded wrong.

When she walked back into the kitchen, her mom looked up immediately.

"What was that?" her mom asked.

Emily's mouth went dry.

"A deputy," she said.

Kate's spoon froze halfway to her mouth.

Her mom's face tightened. "Why is a deputy calling you?"

Emily sat back down, because standing made her feel too visible.

"They got an anonymous report about the reservoir," Emily said. "Henley thought I'd recognize where they meant."

Her mom's eyes flicked to Kate, then back. "Why would she think that?"

Emily's throat tightened.

"Because I've been asking questions," Emily said quietly. "And because people have seen me down there."

Kate's eyes widened. "Clara questions?"

Emily looked at her sister. "Kate—go upstairs."

Kate stiffened. "Why?"

"Because I'm asking you to," Emily said, voice too controlled.

Kate's mouth opened like she wanted to argue. Then she saw their mom's face and thought better of it. She grabbed her bowl and went, slower than she needed to, as if pace could be protest.

When Kate was gone, Emily's mom let out a breath.

"Emily," she said, low and careful. "Have you been going down into the basin?"

Emily didn't answer fast enough.

Her mom's face changed—not dramatic, not theatrical. Just the look of a person realizing a line had been crossed without her permission.

"Tell me the truth," her mom said.

Emily kept her voice steady. "I went down there. I didn't take anything. I didn't touch anything."

Her mom stared at her for a long moment.

Then she looked away, palms flat on the counter like she needed something solid.

"Go to your room," she said. "I need a minute."

Emily didn't argue. She took the stairs.

In her room, she shut the door and sat on the edge of her bed, phone in her hands.

It buzzed.

Blake: deputy at basin. you ok?

Emily stared at it, pulse thudding.

Emily: he called me. henley gave him my name.

A pause.

Then:

Blake: damn.

Blake: zoe ok. home.

Emily swallowed.

Emily: i didn't say anything that points to you.

Blake: good. don't.

Blake: stay inside today. don't go anywhere alone.

Emily set the phone down and stared at the wall.

Outside her window, the sky was bright. The world looked ordinary, like it hadn't been asked to change yet.

Her phone rang again.

Grandpa Tom.

Emily's stomach dropped anyway.

She answered.

"Hi," she said.

Tom didn't waste time with small talk.

"Emmy," he said, voice rougher than usual. "What's going on?"

Emily closed her eyes.

"What did you hear?" she asked.

Tom exhaled slowly. "I've heard your name," he said. "More than once."

Emily's throat tightened.

"Your mom said a deputy called the house," Tom continued. "And that your name is floating around."

Emily swallowed. "I didn't tell anyone my name."

Tom didn't argue with that. He sounded tired, not accusatory.

"Did you go down there?" he asked.

Emily's throat burned.

"Yes," she admitted.

There was a pause long enough to feel.

Tom exhaled slowly, like he was trying to get his hands around something that wouldn't take shape.

Not anger. Not blame.

Just the word someone says when they can't get their hands around a thing.

"I'm coming over," Tom said.

Emily's pulse spiked. "Grandpa—"

"I'm coming over," he repeated. "Not to yell. To be there."

Emily swallowed hard. "Okay."

"Stay inside," Tom added. "And if someone shows up at the door—official or not—you don't handle it alone. You hear me?"

"Yeah," Emily said.

He hung up.

Emily sat on the edge of her bed, hands clenched in her lap.

A few minutes later, her phone buzzed.

An unknown number.

Unknown Number: They're going.

Emily stared at it.

No threat. No comfort.

Just a fact, offered back to her like a mirror.

She didn't respond.

Downstairs, the front door opened and shut.

Footsteps.

Tom's familiar pace.

Her mom's voice, tight and careful: "Dad."

Emily stood and went to the top of the stairs.

Tom was in the entryway with his hat in his hands. He looked like he'd driven straight over without deciding whether that was permission or instinct.

He looked up and saw her.

He didn't climb the stairs. He didn't gesture her down like a child.

He just held her gaze.

Emily went down on her own.

When she reached the last step, Tom moved forward and put a hand on her shoulder—steady, warm, grounding.

"You okay?" he asked.

Emily nodded because it was the only answer she could manage.

Tom glanced toward the kitchen where her mom stood rigid by the counter.

Then he looked back at Emily and lowered his voice.

"Tell me what you told the deputy," he said.

Emily swallowed.

"Just where," she said. "Just what I knew about the Jennings place."

Tom nodded once, absorbing.

His expression wasn't knowing. It wasn't guilty. It was protective and confused in equal measure—the face of a man realizing something buried might be getting pulled up and he doesn't know what it will bring with it.

"Okay," he said quietly. "Then we wait."

Emily's stomach tightened at the word.

Tom seemed to catch it.

"Not the way this town waits," he added. "The way you wait when people are actually on their way."

As if to underline it, Tom's phone rang.

He checked the screen.

"Martha," he said, surprised.

He answered. "Yeah."

He listened.

His face changed—subtle, but immediate.

"No," he said. "I'm with Emmy."

A pause.

Then, quieter: "Yeah. I know."

He hung up and looked at Emily.

"County trucks are headed out," Tom said. "Sheriff too."

Emily's mouth went dry.

Tom's hand stayed on her shoulder.

Not to contain her.

To keep her upright.

Emily stared past him toward the bright morning outside, toward the hills that hid the basin.

Last night she'd pressed send and watched the message disappear.

This morning it was coming back with engines.

And she understood, with a clarity that made her feel hollow:

Truth doesn't arrive like lightning.

It arrives like procedure.

Like phone calls.

Like names traveling faster than facts.

And once your name is in it, you don't get to take it back.

CHAPTER SIXTEEN

Witness Lines

The trucks did not announce themselves.

They arrived the way weather does—first a sound, then a shape, then the certainty that something had already changed.

Emily stood at the living room window, one hand curled into the curtain seam, and watched the first county vehicle roll past. It didn't slow. It didn't look at the house. It just kept going, tires steady on gravel that had already been driven thin by summer traffic.

Grandpa stood a few feet behind her, arms folded, weight set like he was bracing for wind.

"Don't go out," he said.

"I wasn't going to," Emily replied.

Another truck followed. Then a sheriff's vehicle. No lights. No urgency. Just presence.

Emily's phone buzzed.

Zoe: they're blocking the overlook. cones and tape. people already pulling over.

Emily swallowed.

Emily: stay home.

Zoe: trying.

Emily set the phone down.

In the kitchen, her mom moved without speaking. Coffee poured. A mug touched the counter too hard. The radio clicked off.

Kate hovered at the end of the hallway in shorts and an oversized T-shirt, hair still tangled from sleep, not pretending very hard anymore.

"They're really there," Kate said.

Emily didn't turn. "Yeah."

Kate stepped closer. "Why?"

The question wasn't childish. It was exact.

Emily's mom opened her mouth, then closed it again. For a second, Emily thought she would default to *later* or *upstairs* or *don't worry about it*.

Instead, she said, "Because something at the reservoir needs to be checked."

Kate absorbed that. She didn't ask what kind of something.

She nodded once. "Is it bad?"

Emily's chest tightened.

"We don't know yet," Emily said.

Kate looked at her, really looked. "But you're scared."

Emily didn't answer.

Her mom watched them both, then said, more carefully now, "Kate, you don't need details. But you do need to stay close today. No wandering. No going down there. Promise me."

Kate bristled automatically. Then she saw her mom's face.

"I promise," she said, quieter.

She sat down on the arm of the couch instead of disappearing upstairs—close enough to hear, far enough not to intrude.

The house shifted.

Not safer.

Just more honest.

Emily's phone buzzed again.

Blake: sheriff talked to my dad. said it's a "potential site."

Emily stared at the screen.

Emily: does he know who reported it?

A pause.

Blake: no. just "someone."

Emily exhaled.

Emily: you okay?

Another pause.

Blake: ask me later.

Emily set the phone face-down.

Across the street, two neighbors stood talking—Mrs. Calder and her sister, heads bent together. When Mrs. Calder glanced up and saw Emily at the window, she lifted a hand in a half-wave that didn't quite settle on friendliness.

Emily stepped back from the glass.

Grandpa shifted. "I'm going to walk the block."

Emily turned. "Why?"

"To see what kind of day it's turning into," he said. Not a strategy. A habit.

Her mom didn't argue.

Grandpa grabbed his hat and went out.

The house shrank without him.

Emily's phone buzzed.

An unknown number.

She watched it vibrate until it stopped.

Then a text appeared.

Unknown Number: You watching?

Emily's chest tightened.

She didn't respond.

Her mom's voice cut in. "Emily."

Emily turned.

Her mom stood by the counter, arms crossed, eyes sharp with the kind of focus that came before decisions.

"If someone contacts you," she said carefully, "you tell me."

Emily hesitated.

Then nodded. "Okay."

The front door opened again.

Grandpa came back in, slower this time.

"They're keeping people back from the drop," he said. "Asking questions. Mostly curious ones."

Emily swallowed.

"Did anyone ask about me?" she asked.

Grandpa paused just long enough to be honest.

"Someone asked why you weren't out," he said. "I said you were resting."

Emily nodded.

"That still works," Grandpa added. "For now."

Her phone buzzed again.

She picked it up without thinking.

Unknown Number: This isn't how it was supposed to go.

Emily's pulse spiked.

She typed before she could stop herself.

Emily: who is this

The response came immediately.

Unknown Number: Someone who remembers when it was quiet.

Quiet.

Emily thought of the basin—dry, exposed, the water already gone. How long it had been covered without anyone choosing it. How forgetting could feel permanent when nothing disturbed the surface.

Grandpa was watching her.

She shook her head slightly. *Not yet.*

Outside, a siren chirped—not an emergency. Just a marker.

Emily flinched anyway.

Her mom pressed her lips together and said nothing. She didn't reach for a phone. She didn't call anyone. She just stayed where she was, like leaving the room would give something permission to grow.

Grandpa sat down heavily in the armchair.

"They'll bring equipment," he said. "Lights. Barriers. People who know how to look without falling in."

Emily pictured the pale ground, the dark pooled water low and still. The door no longer hidden by depth—only by distance.

Her phone buzzed again.

Zoe: people are saying your name. not blaming. just noticing.

Emily closed her eyes.

Emily: i didn't want that.

Zoe: i know.

A pause.

Zoe: you still did what you thought was right.

Emily wasn't sure she believed in that phrasing anymore.

Grandpa stood again. "I'll make another loop."

Her mom nodded.

Kate shifted on the couch arm but didn't speak.

When Grandpa left, Emily stood in the living room, phone warm in her hand.

Another message came through.

Unknown Number: Quiet kept her safe.

Emily stared at the word.

Her.

The word snagged.

Emily didn't know who *her* was supposed to be.

She didn't know if it meant Clara—or someone else entirely—or if it was just a shape people used when they didn't want to say a name out loud.

The uncertainty felt intentional.

Outside, engines idled. People lingered. Summer held everything open.

And Emily understood something new:

Truth didn't just surface.

Once the water was gone, there was nothing left to cover it.

She set the phone down.

Beyond the hills, the basin waited—bare, watched, unfinished.

And Emily stood in the narrow space between what she knew and what everyone else was about to decide it meant.

CHAPTER SEVENTEEN

First Entry

By the time the tape went up, they didn't let anyone close.

They hadn't planned to leave the house. No one had said *we should go* or *we're allowed to be there*. But by late morning, the air inside had changed—pressure building in corners, voices outside drifting closer than they needed to. Neighbors with nowhere else to be lingered across the street. Someone had knocked once, then apologized for it. Someone else had stood at the end of the driveway pretending to be on their phone, the posture too deliberate to be accidental.

Emily watched it all from the living room window, the glass warm beneath her palm.

Grandpa watched with her for a few minutes, silent, measuring the shape of the day the way he always did. Then he said, "We're not doing this from the window."

Not a question. Not a plan. A boundary.

So they drove.

No one said where they were going out loud. The decision settled into the car without discussion, like gravity. Emily sat in the passenger seat and watched the road slide beneath them, the familiar turns taking on a different weight now that they led somewhere managed. Yesterday, she'd been part of the choosing. Today, she was being carried by it.

Grandpa drove with the window cracked, one hand steady on the wheel, the other resting where it always did, thumb worrying the edge of the leather. He didn't look at Emily, but she felt his awareness of her like a second seatbelt—quiet, present, impossible to ignore.

Kate sat in the back, knees tucked up, gaze fixed on the passing fields. She didn't ask where they were going. She already knew.

The road toward the overlook was crowded with parked trucks and county vehicles, more than Emily had ever seen there at once. A deputy waved them into a gravel pullout short of the turnoff, motion efficient and practiced. Engines idled. Doors opened and shut. People stood beside their cars like no one quite knew what to do with their hands.

From there, the overlook was close enough to see but far enough to control. Yellow tape marked the last stretch, bright and unmistakable against the muted earth tones of late summer.

Emily stepped out of the car and felt the heat rise off the gravel, the smell of dust and sun-baked grass. The air buzzed—not loud, not frantic. Expectant.

She stood with her mom, Grandpa a step behind them, Kate quiet at her elbow. No one told Kate to stay back. No one said this wasn't for kids. She stayed because she understood she was supposed to.

Below them, the basin lay open in the sun.

Not dramatic. Not cinematic.

Just pale ground and darker seams where water still pooled in the lowest places. The Jennings foundation sat off to the side like it always had—half structure, half suggestion. Stone blocks darkened by decades underwater. The outline wrong in a way that was hard to explain if you hadn't stood there before the water dropped.

A small group moved toward it.

Emily counted without meaning to. Two deputies. One man in a vest with a clipboard. Another with a camera slung low against his hip. Gloves. Boots meant for unstable ground. Everything purposeful. Everything chosen.

No one hurried.

"That's deliberate," Grandpa murmured, more to himself than to her.

Emily nodded. She felt it too. The way every step was selected, measured. The absence of rush felt heavier than urgency would have.

Someone stopped near the foundation and crouched. Another held a measuring tape. The man with the clipboard wrote something down, paused, erased it, wrote again.

Kate leaned closer, her shoulder brushing Emily's arm. "Why are they measuring?"

Emily didn't answer right away. The words crowded her throat, jostling for order.

"To mark where things are," her mom said instead. "So nothing gets moved without being recorded."

Kate nodded, absorbing the seriousness of that. The care embedded in the process.

Below, one of the deputies straightened and lifted a hand.

Not a wave. Not a signal of alarm.

Just a pause.

Everyone stopped.

Emily's breath caught. She counted her breaths without meaning to—one, two, three—and stopped when she realized she was waiting for something irreversible. Not confirmation. Permission.

The man with the camera adjusted his angle. The clipboard man looked up.

No one spoke loudly enough for the words to travel.

Then one of them shook his head.

Not no.

Not yes.

Just—not yet.

They moved again.

Emily let out the breath she hadn't realized she was holding, the release leaving her lightheaded. Her knees felt weak, though she was standing still.

A woman in a county jacket approached from the far side of the basin and stopped just short of the foundation. She didn't crouch. She didn't touch anything. She spoke briefly, and the others adjusted without argument, their movements tightening into a new formation.

Kate's fingers brushed Emily's hand.

Emily didn't pull away.

From somewhere behind them, a voice carried—too casual.

"Is it bones?"

The word landed wrong. Too blunt. Too eager.

Emily stiffened.

A deputy turned slowly and met the speaker's eyes. "We're not answering questions right now," he said. Not harsh. Final.

The voice didn't answer back.

Emily felt the weight of that settle—the collective leaning-in, the hunger for a word, a shape, something repeatable. How quickly curiosity sharpened into entitlement.

Down below, one of the deputies carefully cleared a patch of silt with a gloved hand. Slow. Methodical. Like brushing dust off something fragile.

Emily's stomach turned.

She knew where they were. She knew what lay beneath that place.

But watching someone else approach it—official, measured, real—made the knowing feel different. Heavier. Less abstract. Like a thing being transferred from private certainty into public care.

Kate swallowed. "They look nervous."

Emily watched the way the clipboard man's pen paused midair. "Yeah," she said. "They do."

A deputy stepped back and spoke into his radio, voice too low to hear. Another nodded once and turned, scanning the perimeter, gaze methodical.

No sirens. No rush.

Just escalation by inches.

Grandpa shifted behind them. "They'll probably tighten the perimeter," he said. "Once they decide what they're dealing with."

Emily didn't ask who *they* were.

She already knew.

Below, the camera shutter clicked.

Once.

Twice.

Emily flinched at the sound, the sharp mechanical snap cutting through the hush. Her phone buzzed in her pocket, the vibration sudden and intrusive.

She didn't look. She couldn't.

The man with the clipboard straightened and said something to the woman in the county jacket. She listened, then glanced—just once—toward the overlook.

Emily felt it like a physical thing.

Not recognition.

Awareness.

The woman didn't point. Didn't ask. She just turned back and said something sharper, more directive.

The group shifted, forming a loose semicircle around the foundation.

Blocking it.

Protecting it.

Kate whispered, "Does that mean they found something?"

Emily hesitated. The truth pressed at the back of her teeth.

Then she said, carefully, "It means they don't want it disturbed."

Kate nodded. She didn't press. She leaned her weight into Emily's side, trusting without understanding everything she was trusting *about*.

From the road above, another truck pulled in—equipment this time. Lights strapped to the sides. More tape. The boundaries thickening.

Emily's phone buzzed again.

She finally looked.

Unknown Number: They're doing it right.

Emily stared at the words. *Right.* As if there were a correct way for this to unfold. As if rightness could be measured.

She didn't respond. She slid the phone back into her pocket and kept watching.

Down below, the deputy nearest the foundation removed his gloves slowly, like he was aware of his own hands. The man with the clipboard closed his binder.

Not finished.

Paused.

Emily understood then—not with certainty, but with something steadier: whatever was there had crossed a line. Not into truth. But into care.

And once something required care, it could not be pushed back under water.

Kate leaned against Emily's side.

Emily let her.

The sun climbed higher. The basin stayed open.

And the people who knew how to look kept looking.

CHAPTER EIGHTEEN

Chain of Custody

By afternoon, the basin no longer belonged to the town.

Emily could feel the shift without seeing it. The way the road narrowed under cones. The way deputies redirected traffic before anyone had time to argue. The way curiosity started to lose its edge when it met rules instead of rumors. People still craned their necks when they drove past, but the motion had changed—less *What do you know?* and more *What am I allowed to see?*

The pullout where they'd parked earlier was fuller now, but quieter. Fewer voices carrying. More people sitting inside their trucks with the windows cracked, watching like it was a storm line on the horizon—something you didn't approach, but also couldn't look away from.

Grandpa guided them back to the car without saying much. He didn't rush anyone. He didn't comment on what they'd witnessed. He just moved with the firm patience of someone who understood that the longer you stayed near the edge of something, the more it tried to claim you.

Emily followed, her legs heavy, her skin prickling with sun and unease. She kept expecting her body to break into shaking the way it had yesterday, but it didn't. It held. It waited. It stored.

They drove home quietly.

No one said *Did you see that?*

No one said *What do you think they found?*

Kate watched out the window, knees tucked up, chin resting on them like she was trying to memorize the shape of the hills before they changed. Emily sat in the passenger seat this time, her phone heavy in her pocket, silent. She pressed her thumb into the seam of her jeans and focused on that small sensation, as if physical detail could keep her from drifting too far into what-ifs.

Her mom drove with both hands on the wheel, posture steady. The steadiness didn't reassure Emily. It reminded her that adults could drive straight through fear if they had to.

Grandpa sat in the back with Kate, one arm stretched along the bench seat behind her like an unspoken barrier. Not controlling. Just present.

Outside, the town looked the same as it always did. Same sun-bleached lawns. Same flags lifting lazily in the heat. Same trucks parked crooked outside the hardware store.

It felt wrong—how ordinary things insisted on staying ordinary even after you'd learned what was underneath them.

Emily's phone buzzed once.

She didn't take it out.

She knew that if she looked, she'd be consenting to whatever came next. And she needed one more minute where nothing new entered her.

* * *

At home, the house felt different.

Not invaded. Not watched.

Just claimed.

Grandpa locked the door behind them, a small, deliberate click. The sound landed like punctuation.

"That's enough for today," he said, more statement than suggestion.

Emily nodded. Her mom nodded too, like she'd been waiting for someone else to say it so she could accept it without feeling weak.

Her mom set her keys down carefully, like the sound might carry farther than it should. "I'm making food," she said. "We'll eat something normal."

Normal.

Emily didn't trust the word anymore, but she let it exist. She let her mom reach for it like a railing.

Kate looked at Emily. "Can I stay?"

It wasn't a child's question. It wasn't permission-seeking. It was more like *Do we stay together now? Is that the rule?*

Emily met her eyes. "Yeah."

They moved into the kitchen together. Grandpa pulled plates from the cabinet, motions familiar, grounded. Her mom opened the fridge and started gathering—tomatoes, cheese, bread, a leftover container that clinked on the counter.

Ordinary objects. Ordinary sounds.

The kind of domestic choreography that asked the body to remember it still lived in a house and not in a story.

No one turned on the radio.

The silence wasn't empty. It was occupied—by the basin, by the tape, by the careful hands below.

Emily's phone buzzed once.

She didn't take it out.

Her mom sliced bread with more precision than necessary. The knife tapped the cutting board in even rhythms. Grandpa laid out plates like he was setting a table for guests who would arrive late.

Kate stood at the counter with her hands flat on the laminate, watching, absorbing. She asked no questions, but her gaze flicked often to Emily's pocket, where the phone sat like a pulse.

They ate without tasting much.

Not because the food was bad. Because chewing felt like work and swallowing felt like consent. Emily forced herself to finish half a sandwich anyway—because she knew what it meant when her body stopped accepting fuel. Because she didn't want to become weightless again.

When she washed her plate, the warm water soothed her fingers for a second, then left them colder when she pulled away. She dried her hands slowly, mindful of each motion, as if carefulness could be borrowed.

The afternoon slid forward.

Shadows shifted on the floor. The air in the house thickened slightly, heat held by walls that had soaked it up all day. Outside, distant engines came and went—not close enough to identify, but close enough to remind them that the world was still moving.

Emily sat on the couch with Kate beside her, both of them staring at nothing in particular. Grandpa took the armchair like he always did. Her mom moved in and out of the room, tidying without accomplishing anything. She picked up the same magazine twice. Wiped the counter that was already clean. Stood at the window and then turned away as if the glass had offended her.

Emily checked her phone only once, when she couldn't stand the not-knowing anymore.

No messages from the unknown number.

One from Zoe waited in the thread like a held breath.

Zoe: are you ok

Emily didn't answer yet.

Not because she didn't want to.

Because she didn't know what version of okay applied anymore.

*　*　*

The knock came later—soft, deliberate.

Grandpa stood immediately.

"I've got it," he said, already moving.

Emily recognized the sound before she saw her.

Grandma didn't come in quietly.

She didn't rush, either.

She stepped into the house like someone who already knew what kind of room it had become—eyes moving, taking in the air, the stillness, the way everyone had arranged themselves around it.

"Hi," she said.

Not to anyone in particular.

To all of them.

Emily's mom crossed the kitchen first. "Mom."

Grandma opened her arms and held her without asking, one hand firm between her shoulder blades, the other at the back of her head. It wasn't a comfort gesture. It was a stabilizing one.

Then Grandma turned to Kate and Emily.

"Hey," she said again, softer this time.

Emily stood.

Grandma held her just as tightly, forehead resting briefly against Emily's temple. The hug was warm, familiar, unafraid.

"You look tired," Grandma said.

Emily swallowed. "I am."

"That tracks," Grandma said simply.

She didn't ask questions.

She didn't look at the phone.

She didn't scan the windows.

She went straight to the table and sat down like the chair had been waiting for her.

"I brought soup," she said, gesturing toward the bag she'd set down. "And bread. And something sweet I couldn't decide against."

Grandpa exhaled.

Not relief exactly.

Recognition.

They ate again—slowly this time. Not because they were hungry, but because Grandma made it feel allowable to keep the body occupied.

Conversation stayed practical.

What the county had said.

What they hadn't said.

What would probably happen next.

Grandma listened without interrupting, fingers wrapped around her mug.

When Grandpa's phone rang later, she watched his face as he answered.

"Yes," he said.

A pause.

"No. She hasn't been back down there."

Grandma's gaze flicked to Emily—not sharp, not accusing. Protective.

"I understand," Grandpa said.

He hung up.

"They're securing it overnight," he said.

Grandma nodded once. "Good."

"They won't move anything yet."

"Good," she said again.

Kate tilted her head. "You don't sound surprised."

Grandma met her eyes. "I've learned to be patient with people who document before they touch."

Kate nodded. "So... not TV people."

Grandma's mouth curved faintly. "Not those."

* * *

Dusk came without ceremony.

The hills went purple. Then gray. Then disappeared.

From Emily's bedroom window, she could see nothing of the basin—only the dark line of trees and the sky beyond them. No lights. No movement.

That should have felt better.

Instead it made Emily think of all the things that had happened without audience before. How easy it was for silence to pretend it was safety.

Her phone buzzed.

Unknown Number: They won't rush it.

Emily stared at the screen.

Emily: You sound like you know.

The reply took longer this time.

Unknown Number: I know what rushing costs.

Emily didn't respond.

Downstairs, Grandma's voice drifted softly—low, steady, grounding. Not explaining. Just existing.

Emily set the phone down.

For tonight, that was enough.

The house was quiet—not fragile, not tense.

Just held.

CHAPTER NINETEEN

Holding Pattern

The morning after the tape went up, the house stayed quiet on purpose.

Emily woke late, sunlight already pushing through the edges of the blinds. Downstairs, she could hear her mom moving carefully—no radio, no unnecessary noise. The kind of quiet that wasn't about sleep, but about not inviting anything in.

Kate was already awake, sitting cross-legged on the floor with her sketchbook open, pencil moving in short, deliberate strokes.

Emily watched her for a moment.

"You okay?" Emily asked.

Kate nodded without looking up. "I'm just... keeping my hands busy."

Emily understood that instinct too well to question it.

* * *

Grandpa stopped by midmorning.

He didn't stay long. He stood in the kitchen with his hat in his hands, said the county had held overnight like they said they would, said the perimeter was tighter now. He didn't speculate. He didn't try to read ahead.

"They'll call when there's something to call about," he said. "Until then, we let them work."

Emily nodded.

Grandpa looked at her for a moment longer than necessary, then said, "I'll check in later," and let himself out.

When the door closed, the house exhaled again.

* * *

By early afternoon, the quiet started to press.

Not panic. Not fear.

Just the sense that staying inside too long would turn waiting into something heavier.

Emily stood at the front window, watching a car roll past slower than it needed to. Another parked down the street, then moved on. No one knocked. No one waved.

Her mom noticed.

"Don't go toward the basin," she said gently.

"I won't," Emily said.

Her mom nodded. That was enough.

* * *

Emily stepped outside and turned the opposite direction.

Just town.

Just pavement and shade and familiar routes that didn't ask questions.

The air smelled like dust and cut grass. Summer holding where it always had.

She hadn't gone far when Blake came out of the hardware store and saw her.

He hesitated—just a beat—then fell into step beside her.

No greeting. No explanation.

They walked half a block before either of them spoke.

People noticed. Not obviously. A pause in conversation. A glance that didn't linger.

"You don't have to do this," Emily said quietly.

"I know," Blake said.

He didn't say more.

They passed Mrs. Calder again. She nodded this time, watering can lowered, like the moment had already passed inspection.

Blake matched Emily's pace without looking at her. He kept his hands loose at his sides, eyes forward.

"County's being careful," he said finally. "That's good."

Emily nodded. "Yeah."

They walked another block.

Being together didn't make the attention go away. It changed it. Smoothed it into something quieter. Less curious. More settled.

At the corner, Blake slowed.

"I'll head back," he said.

Emily stopped too. "Okay."

He didn't tell her to text.

He didn't say stay safe.

He just turned and crossed the street, leaving her the rest of the walk.

Emily continued on alone.

The town felt steadier now—not kinder, not softer. Just adjusted.

* * *

When she got home, the house was the same as she'd left it.

Kate still on the floor. Her mom at the counter, chopping vegetables.

"You good?" her mom asked.

"Yeah," Emily said. And meant it.

* * *

That night, Emily lay on her bed with the window cracked open, listening to insects buzz in the dark.

Her phone buzzed once.

Unknown Number: They're holding the line.

Emily stared at the message.

Emily: That's their job.

The reply took longer than usual.

Unknown Number: Yes.

Nothing else followed.

Emily set the phone down.

Outside, somewhere beyond the hills, people were working under lights that didn't belong to the town. Writing things down. Measuring. Waiting for authorization.

Inside, the house stayed quiet.

Not hiding.

Just letting the right kind of time pass.

Emily closed her eyes.

The basin had been opened.

The record had begun.

Now came the part no one could rush.

Negative Space

By the third day, the absence of news became its own kind of information.

Emily noticed it first in the way people spoke around her. Not what they said—but what they didn't finish. Sentences that trailed off. Questions softened into statements. Statements left hanging like they were waiting to be contradicted.

At the grocery store, a woman she barely knew said, "At least they're being careful," and didn't specify *about what*.

Emily nodded anyway.

The checkout line took longer than usual. Not because of volume—because of hesitation. People fumbled with wallets they'd used a thousand times. The cashier smiled too carefully.

Outside, the heat sat heavy on the pavement. Summer pressing down, unchanged.

Emily walked home slowly.

* * *

At the house, Kate had taken over the dining table.

Paper spread edge to edge. Rulers. Pencils sharpened down to stubs. She was measuring something again—Emily didn't ask what. She'd learned better than that.

Her mom stood at the sink, hands in soapy water, staring through the window like she was counting something invisible.

"Anything?" Emily asked.

Her mom shook her head. "Nothing."

The word landed flat.

Emily set her keys down. Sat. Watched Kate draw another line and label it with careful numbers.

"What happens if they don't find anything?" Kate asked suddenly.

Emily didn't answer right away.

Her mom turned from the sink. "Then they keep looking until they're sure," she said.

Kate considered this. "And if they do?"

The quiet held.

"Then it gets written down," Emily said finally. "Carefully."

Kate nodded, like that tracked.

She drew another line.

* * *

The fencing remained part of the landscape.

Not new. Not remarked on. Just present in the way rules become present when they don't need explanation anymore. Traffic slowed near it. People adjusted without being told how.

Emily heard about the basin only indirectly now.

A text from Zoe.

Zoe: still nothing official

Zoe: people are acting normal but not really

Emily typed back.

Emily: yeah

Zoe: you holding up?

Emily stared at the screen.

Emily: i'm here

Zoe: okay

* * *

Emily didn't walk that day.

Not because she wasn't allowed.

Because the urge had passed.

Instead, she sat on the porch steps and watched the street.

A county truck rolled by once. Then again. Then not at all.

She thought about Blake—not as a presence this time, but as a deliberate absence. Space given. Distance respected.

She understood that kind of care.

* * *

That evening, Grandpa called.

"I was checking in," he said. Plain. Practical.

"I'm okay," Emily told him.

"I figured," Grandpa said. "You sound steady."

They talked about small things. The heat. A fence line that needed mending. A neighbor who kept losing his gloves.

Nothing circled back.

When they hung up, Emily felt steadier—not comforted, not reassured.

Just anchored.

* * *

The text came after dark.

Unknown Number: Still quiet.

Emily sat on her bed, phone glowing faintly in her hands.

Emily: Quiet doesn't mean anything yet.

The reply took longer than usual.

Unknown Number: No.

Emily waited.

Unknown Number: It just means nothing's been named.

Emily's throat tightened.

Emily: Stop talking like you're part of it.

Three dots appeared.

Disappeared.

Reappeared.

Unknown Number: I know how systems stall.

Emily typed.

Emily: From what?

The dots vanished.

Minutes passed.

Then:

Unknown Number: From deciding too fast.

Emily exhaled slowly.

Emily: Stop circling.

This time, the reply didn't come.

* * *

That night, the house felt fuller.

Not louder. Not warmer.

Just occupied by things that hadn't finished becoming themselves.

Emily lay awake, listening to the quiet spaces between sounds—the refrigerator hum, the click of cooling pipes, the distant bark of a dog she couldn't place.

Negative space, she thought.

The parts that mattered because of what they held back.

Somewhere beyond the hills, people were still measuring. Recording. Writing things down carefully enough that they would last.

Emily had done what she could do.

The rest would take time.

She closed her eyes and let the waiting stretch—not empty, not dramatic.

Just unresolved.

CHAPTER TWENTY ONE

Bare Ground

Emily didn't tell anyone she was going for a walk.

She didn't sneak, exactly. She just didn't announce it. The house had settled into that late-afternoon quiet where nothing felt fragile anymore, just used up. Kate was asleep on the couch with her sketchbook fallen open beside her.

Grandpa stood at the window, hands clasped behind his back, watching the street like it might explain itself.

Her mom had gone upstairs to fold laundry that didn't need folding yet.

Emily grabbed her keys and stepped outside.

The air smelled like dust and warm pine. Summer holding steady.

She made it halfway down the block before she heard footsteps behind her.

"Hey."

She turned.

Blake stood a few yards back, hands shoved into the pockets of his jeans, like he'd been debating whether to say something and lost. He didn't look surprised to see her. Just relieved.

"You stalking me now?" she asked.

He shrugged. "You left with purpose."

"That's rude."

"It's accurate."

She smiled despite herself. "Did Zoe send you?"

"No." He paused. "I just figured you'd need to move."

Emily considered that. Then nodded. "Yeah."

They fell into step together, heading nowhere in particular. Past houses with open windows. Past sprinklers ticking across lawns. The town looked like itself again—ordinary, careful, pretending it hadn't held its breath all day.

They walked in silence for half a block before Emily noticed.

"Blake," she said, slowing.

He stopped. "Yeah?"

She looked down.

"You're not wearing shoes."

He glanced at his feet like this was new information. "Huh."

"You're going to step on something awful," Emily said. "Glass. A nail. A very judgmental pinecone."

He huffed a quiet laugh. "Pinecones are aggressive."

"I'm serious," she said. "This town is ninety percent sharp objects pretending to be scenery."

He shrugged, unbothered. "I watch where I step."

"That is not the same thing as wearing shoes."

He tilted his head, studying her. "You worried about me?"

Emily rolled her eyes. "I don't want to have to explain to anyone that you got tetanus while walking dramatically."

That did it. He smiled—quick, unguarded.

"I forgot them," he said. "Didn't feel like going back."

She stared at him for a second. Then down at her own sneakers.

"You always do this when you're thinking," she said.

"Do what?"

"Forget you have feet."

Blake considered that. "Fair."

They walked another few steps. Emily's attention kept snagging on the sound—his bare feet against the pavement, soft and sure. It was strange how familiar it felt, like noticing something that had always been true and just hadn't mattered until now.

She stopped again.

"This is ridiculous," she muttered.

Then she stepped off to the side, tugged her shoes off, and looped the laces together.

Blake blinked. "What are you doing?"

"If you're going to step on something awful," she said, "I'm not letting you do it alone."

His eyebrows lifted. "That's not how risk mitigation works."

"Don't care."

She stepped back onto the sidewalk barefoot.

The concrete was warm. Grit pressed into the pads of her feet. Real in a way shoes kept you from noticing.

Blake watched her for a moment, something careful passing across his face.

"You don't have to," he said.

"I know," Emily said. "I just want to."

They started walking again.

Neither of them said anything about it.

Something in the space between them loosened anyway.

They turned down a quieter street, one that curved instead of cutting straight through. The kind of road people used when they weren't in a hurry.

"You okay?" Blake asked after a while.

Emily thought about lying. Thought about saying fine the way people expected.

"I don't know," she said instead. "But I don't feel like I'm going to fall over anymore."

He nodded. "That counts."

They walked another block.

"Everyone's going to have opinions," Blake said. "About today. About what should happen next."

"I know."

"They already do."

Emily exhaled. "I hate that part."

"Yeah." He scuffed his foot lightly against the pavement. "Me too."

She glanced at him. "You don't have to keep doing this. Walking me. Showing up."

"I know," he said.

That stopped her.

She looked at him fully this time.

"Then why are you?" she asked.

Blake didn't answer right away. He watched the street ahead, the curve of it disappearing behind cottonwoods.

"Because," he said finally, "you didn't turn it into a spectacle."

Emily frowned. "I didn't do anything special."

"You did," he said quietly. "You let it become work. Paper. Process. You didn't make it about you."

She swallowed. "It didn't feel like a choice."

"Those are usually the real ones," he said.

They slowed near the end of the block. Not stopping. Just easing.

The ground under Emily's feet was rougher here. Gravel scattered from a recent repair. She adjusted without thinking, stepping where it was smoother.

Blake noticed.

"See?" he said. "You watch where you step."

She snorted. "Don't push it."

They stood there for a moment longer than necessary.

Blake shifted his weight. "I should head back."

"Yeah," Emily said. "Me too."

Neither of them moved right away.

Then Emily slipped her shoes back on, the laces gritty with dust. Blake stayed barefoot, unbothered.

"I'll walk you to your place," he said.

She didn't argue.

When they reached her driveway, Blake stopped at the edge of it—not on the concrete, not on the grass. Like he knew where to pause.

"Text me if it gets loud," he said. "Not sirens. People."

Emily nodded. "You too."

He hesitated, then added, "You don't have to carry all of it."

"I know," she said again.

This time, it felt closer to true.

Blake stepped back, barefoot on familiar ground, and turned away.

Emily watched him go, then went inside.

The house was still quiet. Still held.

She kicked her shoes off by the door and didn't put them back on.

Just stood there for a second, feeling the floor beneath her feet.

Solid.

Still there.

CHAPTER TWENTY TWO

Correction

Emily's mom stood at the counter with a short list in her hand, the pen hovering like she was considering adding something just to make it feel finished.

Finally, she tore the page off and slid it across the counter.

"Take this," she said. "And don't rush."

Emily glanced down. Bread. Milk. potatoes. Ordinary. Contained.

Her mom met her eyes. "I need you to have something to do."

Emily nodded. "Okay."

Outside, the day had moved on without asking. Cars passed. Someone down the block started a lawnmower and stopped it again. Nothing marked the morning as different except the way people watched one another, like everyone was waiting for the same thing to be said out loud.

The grocery store was busy in a careful way. Conversations stayed low. People spoke in fragments, glancing toward the door as if they expected someone official to walk in and settle it.

No one had said anything yet.

Emily grabbed a basket and focused on the list because it had an end.

Near the dairy case, she heard her name.

"Emily."

She turned.

Grandma stood a few feet away with a cart, one hand resting on the handle. Her hair was pinned back, cardigan buttoned. Ready for being seen.

"Hi, Grandma," Emily said.

Grandma nodded once. "Your mom send you out?"

"Yeah. Gave me a job."

"Good," Grandma said. "People need one right now."

They moved through the aisle together without comment.

At the checkout lanes, a voice carried farther than it should have.

"They still haven't said anything," someone murmured.

"No official word."

"But everybody knows."

Another voice followed, sharper.

"She always wanted more than this place," a woman said. "That's what my mom used to say. Too big for it. Difficult, even when she was young."

Emily stopped.

Grandma took one more step. Then turned.

"Clara had plans," she said evenly. "That's not the same as being careless."

The woman blinked. "I just meant—"

"She pushed," Grandma continued. "She argued. She wanted more than what was offered." Grandma met the woman's eyes. "None of that makes this inevitable."

The space between them went quiet.

No one rushed to fill it.

"She was my friend," Grandma said, not loudly. Not defensively. Just as fact.

Then she adjusted the cart handle.

"She always took her shoes off at the door," she said. "Even if she was angry. Even if she meant to leave again."

The woman stared at her, uncertain.

"She liked to feel where she was," Grandma added.

Then Grandma turned back to the cooler, took out a carton of milk, and placed it in the cart.

That was the end of it.

Outside, the parking lot shimmered with heat. They crossed it side by side, not touching.

"You didn't have to say anything," Emily said.

"Yes," Grandma said. "I did."

They reached the end of the driveway and stopped.

"I won't correct every version," Grandma said. "But I won't let her be reduced."

Emily nodded. "I'm glad you said it."

Grandma's mouth tightened slightly. Not a smile. Something steadier.

"You did what you needed to do," she said. "Now let the rest unfold."

She turned and walked back toward her car.

Inside the house, Emily set the groceries on the counter. Her mom took them without comment, checking items off the list like this was a normal afternoon.

Kate sat at the table, drawing the same rectangle again, darker now, more deliberate.

"You went out," Kate said, without looking up.

"Yeah."

Kate glanced up. "People are saying her name again."

Emily nodded. "They are."

Kate went back to her drawing. "They always do that before they know anything."

Emily leaned against the counter.

The errand was finished. The reason for being out already gone.

Outside, the town kept talking.

Still no statement.

Still no confirmation.

Just a name moving faster than the truth.

CHAPTER TWENTY THREE

Held Ground

By the fourth day, the town had learned how to wait without admitting that was what it was doing.

No announcements.

No confirmations.

Just the slow recalibration of routine around an absence that hadn't been named yet.

Emily felt it in the way people paused before speaking. In the careful neutrality that settled over her name. In the way silence itself seemed to have rules now.

By midafternoon, the house felt full of it.

Her mom folded laundry that didn't need folding. Kate lay on the living room floor with her sketchbook, the same rectangle darkened again, edges reinforced. Grandpa stopped by briefly with a bag of cherries and left without sitting down.

"Anything?" Emily asked.

Grandpa shook his head. "Nothing official."

That phrase stayed with her.

Emily waited until the quiet inside her chest tipped from manageable into restless. Not panic. Not urgency. Just the familiar pull—the sense that if she didn't move, something in her would start pacing without her.

She grabbed her keys.

No announcement. No explanation. Her mom looked up from the counter and nodded once, like she understood exactly what was being managed.

At the fork in the road, Emily turned right.

Left led to the basin—to fencing and county trucks and the weight of being watched.

Right followed the river as it always had.

She parked at the small pullout where people stopped when they wanted sound instead of answers.

The river was high but steady, water sliding over rock in a continuous, unbothered motion. It hadn't changed its mind. It hadn't revealed anything. It just moved.

Emily stood at the edge for a long moment, shoes still on, letting the sound pull her breathing back into something even.

Footsteps crunched on gravel behind her.

She didn't turn.

"You're going to step on something awful," she said.

Blake stopped beside her. She could hear him glance down.

"They toughen up," he said.

Emily didn't look at him. "That's not how feet work."

There was a brief pause.

She glanced over despite herself.

Blake gave a lopsided grin and a small shrug, like being corrected didn't cost him anything.

Something in Emily's chest shifted. Not relief. Not warmth.

Attention.

She looked back to the water first, annoyed that she'd noticed at all.

She didn't ask how he knew. Blake had always known which way she turned when the noise got loud.

The river kept moving.

Blake didn't say anything else. He didn't fill the space or explain himself. He just stood there, close enough that Emily could feel the warmth of him without turning.

She hesitated.

Then, deliberately, she leaned slightly into him—not enough to be obvious, not enough to ask for anything. Just contact. Chosen.

Blake didn't move away. He didn't adjust or comment. He simply stayed, steady as the ground beneath them.

They stood there together at the edge, saying nothing.

Emily bent and untied her shoes. Socks too. She folded them together and set them on a dry rock, deliberate as if she were putting something down, not taking it off.

The ground was cool under her feet. Gritty. Uneven.

Only then did she step into the water.

The cold snapped her fully into herself. Her breath caught, then evened out as the current slid around her ankles.

She exhaled.

Blake watched without comment.

"Better?" he asked quietly.

"Yeah," she said. "Much."

They stayed like that a little longer, the river doing what it did best—moving without asking permission.

When they finally stepped back onto the bank, Emily picked up her shoes and socks and carried them instead of putting them on. Blake noticed and said nothing.

They walked toward the cars slowly.

At the edge of the lot, Blake stopped.

"You hungry?" he asked.

Emily thought about the house. About the waiting there.

"Yeah," she said. "I think so."

"Dairy Queen?" he offered. Not tentative. Not insistent. Just normal.

She nodded. "Okay."

He smiled—smaller this time, steadier.

As they headed back toward their cars, Emily glanced down at his bare feet.

"You're still going to step on something awful," she said.

Blake shrugged. "Probably."

She didn't smile.

But she felt lighter as she drove away from the river, shoes on the floor of the passenger seat, water still cooling her skin.

The town was still waiting.

The truth was still unfinished.

But she knew where she was.

And she knew who could stand beside her while she stayed there.

For now, that was enough.

CHAPTER TWENTY FOUR

Normal Hours

Emily pulled into the Dairy Queen lot and cut the engine.

A second later, Blake's truck rolled in beside hers and parked close enough that she could hear the tick of his engine cooling after he shut it off. It felt intentional. Not crowding. Just there.

She glanced down at the passenger floorboard, where her shoes sat tangled together, socks folded inside them. She left them there.

Blake noticed. Said nothing.

They ordered burgers at the walk-up window and carried the paper baskets to one of the outdoor tables. The metal bench was warm beneath Emily's thighs. Her bare feet pressed against the rough concrete, still cool in places from the river.

She pulled out her phone.

Emily: not coming home for dinner

Emily: at dairy queen

Emily: with blake

The typing dots appeared. Paused. Appeared again.

Mom: okay

Mom: just don't go near the reservoir

Mom: text when you're done

Emily exhaled and typed back.

Emily: i won't

Emily: i will

They ate without rushing. Grease soaked through the paper. Ketchup smeared one of Emily's fingers, and she wiped it on a napkin instead of her jeans. It felt good to focus on something ordinary that required attention.

People came and went. A group of middle school kids crowded the window. A couple leaned against the fence, arguing quietly about fries.

No one stared.

Her phone buzzed.

Zoe.

Zoe: alive?

Emily smiled and typed.

Emily: yeah

Emily: dairy queen

Emily: burgers

Zoe: with him?

Emily paused — not because she didn't want to say it, but because it felt newly specific.

Emily: yeah

Zoe: ok

Zoe: come by after

Zoe: i'm home

Emily locked her phone and set it face down.

Then she picked it up again and typed.

Emily: heading to zoe's after

Emily: should be home later

The reply came quickly.

Mom: okay

Mom: drive safe

Emily let out a breath she hadn't realized she was holding and slid the phone back into her pocket.

Blake finished his burger and wiped his hands on a napkin.

"You need to head out soon?"

"Yeah," Emily said. "Before Zoe starts narrating my disappearance."

Blake huffed a quiet breath of a laugh. "That sounds about right."

"I'll follow you," he added.

She didn't argue.

They drove back through town, Blake's truck steady in her rearview mirror. When Emily turned onto Zoe's street, he stayed with her, pulling in behind her when she parked.

He got out as she shut her door.

Emily noticed his feet immediately.

"You're still barefoot," she said. "You're going to step on something awful."

Blake glanced down at her bare feet and gave a quick, crooked grin. "We're consistent."

He shrugged like that settled it.

"I'll grab my shoes," Emily said, bending to scoop them off the passenger floorboard.

Blake nodded. "Text me when you're done. Or if it gets loud."

"I will."

He hesitated, then said, quieter, "I'm glad you got out today."

Not praise. Not judgment. Just presence.

Blake walked back to his truck and drove off.

Emily carried her shoes up Zoe's steps.

Zoe opened the door in socks, popcorn bowl already in hand.

"I was about to start a missing-person narrative," Zoe said.

Emily huffed a breath. "You knew where I was."

"Yeah. Forever ago." Zoe's eyes dropped to Emily's feet. "River?"

"Yeah."

Zoe stepped aside. "That tracks."

They settled onto the couch, knees angled away but close, the familiar geometry of them. Zoe didn't rush her. That mattered.

After a few minutes, Emily said, "My grandma corrected someone at the store today."

Zoe looked up. "About Clara?"

"Yeah. Someone was repeating the old stuff — difficult, too big for this place. Grandma shut it down."

Zoe's mouth tightened. "Good."

"She said Clara was her friend," Emily added. "And that she always took her shoes off at the door. Even when she was angry."

Zoe blinked. "That's... specific."

"Yeah."

They sat with it.

Outside, the town kept talking — faster than facts, louder than truth.

Inside, Emily stayed barefoot on the rug, her shoes abandoned by the door.

For now, that was enough.

CHAPTER TWENTY FIVE

Pressure Points

Zoe didn't push right away.

That was how Emily knew she was going to.

They sat on the floor this time, backs against the couch, popcorn between them. The TV stayed dark. Zoe ate slowly, deliberately, like she was measuring the space Emily was taking up.

Emily waited.

Finally, Zoe said, "You're doing the thing."

Emily didn't look over. "What thing?"

"The calm thing," Zoe said. "Where you become extremely reasonable so nobody can argue with you."

Emily exhaled. "I'm just tired."

"I know," Zoe said. She tipped her head back against the couch. "That's why it's concerning."

Emily smiled despite herself. "You always say that."

"Because it keeps being true."

They were quiet for a minute. The house creaked as it settled. Someone walked past outside, footsteps slowing, then moving on.

Zoe nudged the popcorn bowl toward Emily. "You don't have to explain anything," she said. "But you also don't get to disappear into logistics again."

Emily's throat tightened. She hated that Zoe knew the name of it.

"I'm not disappearing," Emily said.

Zoe looked at her then. Not sharp. Just steady. "You went to the river. You went barefoot. You ate a burger like it was an assignment. You're managing."

Emily picked up a kernel and crushed it between her fingers. "Someone has to."

Zoe didn't answer right away.

Then: "You're allowed to be scared."

The word landed harder than Emily expected.

"I'm not—" she started.

Zoe cut her off gently. "I didn't say falling apart. I said scared."

Emily's eyes burned. She blinked hard and looked at the floor.

"I don't know what I'm supposed to do with that," she said.

Zoe leaned back again. "Nothing. You just don't pretend it's not there."

Emily nodded once. She could do that much.

Her phone buzzed.

She didn't pick it up right away.

Zoe noticed anyway. "Who is it?"

Emily checked the screen.

Blake: you good?

Emily hesitated, then typed.

Emily: yeah

Emily: at zoe's

Three dots appeared almost immediately.

Blake: want company or quiet?

Emily stared at the question.

Zoe tilted her head. "Company doesn't have to mean me."

Emily swallowed.

Emily: company

The reply came fast.

Blake: ok

Blake: be there in a bit

Emily set the phone down.

Zoe raised an eyebrow. "You invited him over."

Emily stared at the wall. "I didn't invite him. I answered a question."

Zoe smiled, just slightly. "Sure."

They waited.

Emily didn't pace. Didn't rehearse. She let the time pass like water moving around her instead of over her.

When Blake knocked, Zoe got up without being asked.

"I'm making tea," she said. "You want some?"

"Yes," Blake said. "Please."

Zoe disappeared into the kitchen.

Blake stood there for a second, unsure, then stepped fully inside.

He glanced down.

Emily was still barefoot.

"So," he said lightly. "Consistent."

She huffed a breath. "You're going to get us both tetanus."

He smiled, but his eyes stayed on her face this time. "You okay?"

Emily nodded auGrandpaatically.

Then shook her head.

"No," she said. "But I'm not breaking."

Blake nodded like that made sense.

He sat on the floor beside her without asking, close enough that his shoulder brushed hers. He didn't apologize for the contact. Didn't exaggerate it.

Just there.

Emily leaned into him.

It surprised them both.

Blake stilled, then adjusted slightly, letting her weight settle. His arm came up, resting along the back of the couch — not around her, not holding.

Grounding without containment.

Zoe came back with three mugs and paused.

She clocked the posture. The proximity. The way Emily hadn't pulled away.

"Okay," Zoe said. "I see the situation."

Emily didn't move. "You're not allowed to make this weird."

"I'm not," Zoe said. "I'm allowed to be relieved."

She handed them their mugs and sat back down across from them.

They drank in silence for a minute.

Then Zoe said, "If people stop talking about process," she said carefully, "and start talking about you — you don't do it alone."

Emily glanced at Blake, then back at Zoe.

"I won't," she said.

Zoe's shoulders eased, just a little.

Outside, a car passed. Somewhere down the street, someone laughed — a sound that didn't belong to this moment and existed anyway.

Emily rested her head briefly against Blake's shoulder.

Just long enough to feel steady.

Then she straightened.

"Okay," she said. "I think I can sleep tonight."

Zoe smiled. "Look at that. Progress."

Blake didn't move right away.

"Text me when you're home," he said.

Emily nodded. "I will."

For once, it didn't feel like a promise she'd have to force herself to keep.

CHAPTER TWENTY SIX

Attention

Emily found Grandma in the kitchen, sorting through mail at the small table by the window.

Not cooking. Not cleaning. Just aligning envelopes into neat piles like she was deciding what deserved to be opened at all. Late-afternoon light slanted across the linoleum, catching the edge of the table.

"I dropped off the bread," Emily said, holding up the bag.

Grandma nodded without looking up. "Set it there."

Emily did — and only then noticed she was barefoot again. The floor was cool beneath her heels.

Grandma noticed too.

Her gaze dipped briefly. Not lingering. Just noting.

"You always do that," she said.

Emily frowned. "Do what?"

"Take your shoes off when you're thinking," Grandma said. Not accusing. Just precise. "Not because you forgot them. Because you chose to."

Emily shifted her weight. "It helps."

Grandma nodded once, like that confirmed something instead of explaining it.

"Clara did that," she said, sliding an envelope open. "Said she needed to feel where she was standing."

Emily's throat tightened. "I didn't know that."

"No," Grandma said. "Most people didn't."

She read the contents of the envelope, folded the paper once, and set it aside.

"She wasn't careless," Grandma went on. "She was attentive. There's a difference people like to ignore."

Emily leaned against the counter, careful not to interrupt.

"She'd take her shoes off before an argument," Grandma said. "Drove her mother crazy. Everyone thought it was defiance."

She looked up then — just long enough to make sure Emily was listening.

"It wasn't," she said. "It was focus."

Emily swallowed. "People keep saying she was difficult."

Grandma's mouth tightened. Not angry. Settled.

"People call women difficult when they won't dull themselves to make things easier," she said. "Especially here."

She picked up her mug and took a sip that had long since gone cold.

"Shoes make it easier not to notice what's under you," Grandma added. "Some people can't afford that."

Something settled in Emily's chest. Not comfort. Recognition.

"I don't think I'm brave," Emily said quietly.

Grandma studied her for a long moment.

"Neither did Clara," she said. "She just didn't stop paying attention."

A car passed outside. Gravel crunching. Ordinary sound.

Grandma gathered the mail and tucked it into a drawer.

"You should head home," she said, reaching for the kettle. "It's getting late."

Emily nodded.

At the door, she slipped her shoes on, slower than she needed to.

Grandma didn't comment.

As Emily stepped out onto the porch, Grandma spoke again — not looking up.

"Being aware doesn't keep you safe," she said. "But it keeps you honest."

Emily paused, then nodded once.
She walked down the steps and back toward her truck.
The shoes felt wrong for a few seconds.
Then she adjusted.

CHAPTER TWENTY SEVEN

Orientation

The parking lot was already half full.

Not crowded—just busy in the way places get when people didn't know where they were supposed to be yet. Cars idled. Doors opened and shut. Groups formed and re-formed, like everyone was pretending not to look for someone specific.

Senior Orientation, the sign said, taped crookedly to the front doors.

Emily parked between a dented Subaru and a newer SUV that still looked like it belonged somewhere else. She cut the engine and sat there for a second longer than necessary.

"You ready?" Zoe asked.

Emily nodded. "Yeah."

She wasn't, but that didn't feel like a useful distinction.

They got out. The air had shifted overnight—not cold, not warm. Just different. Summer thinning. The kind of morning that made you notice your breath if you tried.

Emily had put her shoes on. She noticed immediately how much she hated it.

Blake came up behind them from the far row, backpack slung over one shoulder. He didn't wave. Just fell into step like that was where he'd been headed anyway.

Zoe clocked it and said nothing.

They walked toward the building together.

Emily felt it before she could name it—the pause in a conversation to her left. The way two girls by the curb glanced over and then looked away too quickly.

Zoe noticed a beat later.

"Oh," she murmured. "Okay."

Emily frowned. "What?"

Zoe didn't answer right away. Her eyes tracked a cluster near the doors, voices low, bodies angled inward.

"That," Zoe said quietly. "That's new."

A boy Emily didn't know passed them and didn't nod.

Emily's sGrandpaach tightened.

Blake's hand brushed the back of her arm. Not a grip. A question.

Emily let her shoulders drop.

Someone behind them said, not quite quietly, "You heard?"

Another voice answered, "Yeah."

No names. No context. Just enough.

Emily hadn't done anything.

Zoe stopped walking.

"Nope," Zoe said. "We're not doing the thing where you pretend that didn't happen."

Emily kept her voice low. "I don't want this to turn into—"

"Into what?" Zoe asked. "People knowing you exist?"

Emily swallowed.

Blake stepped closer, shoulder to shoulder now. His fingers found her wrist, light pressure on the inside. Grounding. Familiar.

Emily focused on the feel of it. The steady pulse there. Her own.

"They're not mad," Zoe said, reading the lot like a map. "They're curious. Which is worse."

Emily huffed a breath. "Fantastic."

A girl from the soccer team walked past and hesitated.

"Hey, Emily."

"Hey."

The girl nodded, then tilted her head. "You okay?"

Emily opened her mouth.

Blake's hand stayed where it was.

"Yeah," Emily said. "Just orientation."

The girl nodded again, uncertain, and moved on.

Zoe watched her go. "See? That's the shift."

Emily stared at the doors. The sign flapping slightly in the breeze. The building smelled wrong already—no lockers open, no bells. Like a place waiting to become itself again.

"I don't know how to stop noticing," Emily said.

Blake spoke quietly. "You don't."

Emily looked at him.

"You just decide who's close when it gets loud," he said.

Zoe nodded once. "Exactly."

A group ahead of them started moving inside. Someone laughed too hard. Someone else checked their phone like it might explain things.

Emily took a breath.

Then another.

She leaned slightly into Blake. Not because she was falling. Because she chose to.

Zoe saw it and didn't comment.

"That works," Zoe said instead. "We'll adjust."

Emily nodded.

They moved with the rest of them, into the building, into the year that had already started to claim her name.

Behind them, the parking lot kept talking.

"You heard?"

"Yeah."

Emily heard it too.

She just didn't turn around.

CHAPTER TWENTY EIGHT

Official

The announcement didn't arrive all at once.

Emily heard it first on the radio while her mom stood at the counter with a mug she wasn't drinking.

"...Beaverhead County officials confirmed this morning—"

Emily stopped halfway down the stairs.

Her mom didn't turn the volume up. She didn't turn it off either.

"...human remains were located during a controlled site inspection at Pine Valley Reservoir. Authorities believe the remains are associated with a historical missing-person case reported in 1965. Identification is pending. The site remains secured."

No name.

Not yet.

Emily stepped back up the last stair and sat on the edge of her bed, pressing her palms to her thighs until the room stopped tilting.

Her phone buzzed.

A county alert.

BCSO UPDATE: *Human remains located during inspection at Pine Valley Reservoir. Believed to be associated with a historical missing-person case. Investigation ongoing.*

Still no name.

Her phone buzzed again.

Zoe: it's on the radio

Zoe: fb is already doing what fb does

Zoe: you okay

Emily stared at the wall for a moment longer than necessary.

Emily: i'm here

Zoe: good

Zoe: i'm heading into town later

Emily set the phone face-down.

Downstairs, her mom cleared her throat softly, like she didn't want to startle anything.

"Do you still need to go in today?" she asked.

Emily nodded. "Yeah. My schedule's wrong."

Her mom turned. "Wrong how?"

"I've got World History. I'm supposed to have Civics."

Her mom exhaled. Not relieved — just glad there was something concrete to fix.

"Okay," she said. "Take the truck."

* * *

The school parking lot was half full in a way that felt temporary.

Cars angled slightly wrong. People standing beside open doors, comparing papers. Teachers moved through the space with clipboards instead of lesson plans.

No bells. No urgency. Just motion.

Emily held her printed schedule like it might change again if she looked away.

World History. Third period. Wrong.

Inside, the commons had a TV mounted high in one corner, volume off. A local news banner crawled beneath a still image of the reservoir dam.

INVESTIGATION ONGOING — NO OFFICIAL IDENTIFICATION YET

Clusters formed beneath it anyway.

Emily heard fragments as she passed.

"They basically said—"

"My cousin swears—"

"They haven't named her but—"

Blake fell into step beside her before she saw him.

"You going to counseling?" he asked quietly.

She nodded. "Schedule fix."

"Yeah," he said. "They screwed up senior schedules."

Emily glanced at him. "How bad?"

"Civics didn't land where it was supposed to," he said. "A bunch of people got dropped into random classes."

She exhaled. "That tracks."

Zoe appeared on her other side, papers tucked under her arm.

"Okay," Zoe said. "So it's not just you."

They moved together toward the counseling office.

***

The line was slow. Not because there were so many people — because no one quite knew what to say while they waited.

A counselor stepped out, spoke low to a parent, nodded, disappeared again.

Someone's phone chimed with another alert.

Emily didn't look.

Blake shifted closer, his hand finding her wrist. Not gripping. Just there.

"Still summer," he murmured. "Still not classes."

She breathed.

When it was her turn, she slid the schedule through the window.

"This should be Civics," she said. "Not World History."

The counselor glanced down, typed, frowned once, then nodded.

"You're right," she said. "That's our error."

Click. Click.

She slid a corrected schedule back.

Civics.

Third period.

"Anything else?" the counselor asked.

Emily shook her head.

Outside the office, Zoe leaned in. "Fixed?"

Emily nodded.

"Good," Zoe said. "One thing behaving like it's supposed to."

* * *

They stepped back into the commons.

The TV image had changed — still no footage from the site, just the dam from a different angle. The banner remained careful. Conditional.

No name.

A teacher crossed herself quietly near the doors.

Someone else said, "So it really was her."

Another voice replied, "They didn't say that."

Emily felt it land — not as shock, but as gravity.

Blake's thumb pressed once at her wrist.

Zoe didn't speak. She just stayed close.

* * *

Outside, the heat sat heavy in the parking lot.

"So," Zoe said finally. "We've got official-but-not-official."

Emily nodded. "They're letting the system speak first."

"That's how they do it," Blake said.

Emily folded the corrected schedule and slid it into her bag.

"She's not missing anymore," she said quietly.

Zoe's mouth tightened. "No."

They stood there for a moment longer than necessary.

Blake tilted his head toward the street. "You want company?"

Zoe tilted hers the other way. "Company doesn't have to mean me."

Emily thought about the radio. The alert. The scrolling banner. The way the name still hovered, unsaid.

"Walk with me," she said.

Blake smiled — small, steady.

"Yeah," he said. "Always."

They moved away from the building, the school behind them still waiting to become what it would be.

The truth had entered the system.

It just hadn't finished finding its words yet.

CHAPTER TWENTY NINE

Named

The name didn't come from the radio.

Emily realized that later—after she tried to remember where she'd first heard it spoken out loud and couldn't.

It came the way truth often does in small towns: sideways.

She was in the kitchen with Zoe, the two of them leaning against opposite counters while Emily's mom stood at the sink rinsing grapes she didn't seem in a hurry to eat. The house was quiet in that late-afternoon way, light slanting through the window like it was testing where it could land.

Zoe's phone buzzed.

She glanced at it. Froze.

Emily felt it before Zoe said anything—the way the air shifted, subtle but unmistakable.

"They released it," Zoe said.

Emily didn't ask what.

Her mom turned slowly from the sink.

"Released what?" she asked, already knowing.

Zoe swallowed. "The identification."

Emily's pulse thudded once, hard enough to feel in her throat.

Her mom reached for a towel and dried her hands carefully, like she needed something to do with them.

Zoe looked at Emily. "It's Clara Jennings."

The name settled.

Not sharp. Not explosive.

Heavy. Final.

Emily closed her eyes.

When she opened them again, nothing had changed in the room. The counter was still cool beneath her palms. The clock still ticked. Outside, a car passed like it always did.

Her mom pressed a hand to her mouth—not to stop herself from speaking, but like the name had knocked the breath out of her.

"Oh," she said quietly.

Zoe nodded. "They said dental records. Personal effects. Enough to be sure."

Emily's sGrandpaach tightened at the phrase personal effects.

Her mom leaned back against the counter. "How are they saying it?"

Zoe glanced down at her phone again. "Careful. Historical case. No speculation. They're emphasizing time elapsed."

Time elapsed.

Like Clara had simply been misplaced for a while.

Emily's phone buzzed.

She already knew who it would be.

Blake: they named her

Blake: you want me there

Emily didn't answer right away.

Her mom looked at her then. Really looked.

"You don't have to be alone with this," she said.

Emily nodded. "I know."

She typed.

Emily: yeah

The reply came almost immediately.

Blake: on my way

Zoe let out a breath she'd been holding. "Okay," she said. "Good."

Emily looked at her. "You don't have to stay."

Zoe tilted her head. "Company doesn't have to mean me."

Then, softer: "But it can."

Emily nodded.

They didn't turn on the radio.

They didn't refresh their phones.

They let the house hold the moment the way it had learned to.

When Blake arrived, he didn't knock right away. He waited just long enough that Emily could choose to open the door instead of feeling like it was opened for her.

He stood on the porch, barefoot again, like the world hadn't reorganized itself just because a name had been confirmed.

Emily noticed immediately.

"You're still barefoot," she said.

"You're going to step on something awful."

He glanced down, then at her feet—still bare from earlier—and gave that quick, lopsided grin.

"Occupational hazard," he said.

She huffed something that wasn't quite a laugh and stepped aside to let him in.

He didn't say I'm sorry.

He didn't say anything at all.

He just reached for her wrist, steady and familiar, grounding her back into her body.

Inside, Zoe watched them with a look Emily couldn't quite read—not jealousy, not distance. Something like relief.

"That's her," Zoe said quietly, for Blake's sake.

"I know," he said.

Emily leaned into him then—just slightly. Enough to be intentional.

Outside, the town was already adjusting.

Names were being spoken again. Headlines updated. Conversations recalibrated.

Inside the house, no one rushed.

Clara Jennings was no longer a question.

She was a record now.

And for the first time since the water receded, Emily felt the shift she'd been bracing for—not toward resolution, but toward consequence.

The story had been named.

What came next would have to be lived.

CHAPTER THIRTY

After the Name

After the name was spoken, the town behaved like it had completed something.

Emily noticed it the next morning.

People said good morning again. Not carefully. Not sideways. Just good morning, like the words had been waiting to be used. A man waved from across the street. Someone else asked her mom if she needed anything from the store.

Not sympathy.

Normalcy.

That was the shift.

Emily stood at the sink rinsing a mug she hadn't used, listening to her mom talk quietly on the phone in the other room. Not about Clara. About groceries. About schedules. About whether it was still too hot to bake.

Life making its case.

Her phone buzzed.

Blake: you want out of the house

Emily stared at the screen for a moment.

Emily: yeah

Blake: five minutes

She slipped on her shoes, grabbed her keys, and stepped onto the porch just as Blake's truck rolled to a stop at the end of the driveway.

He leaned across the bench seat and pushed the door open for her.

"Morning," he said.

"You're barefoot," she said immediately.

"You're going to step on something awful."

He glanced down at his feet, then back up at her, unfazed.

"Hasn't happened yet."

She climbed in, shaking her head.

They drove out of town without talking much. Dust kicked up behind them, then settled. At the split in the road, Blake turned right—toward the river, not the reservoir.

Emily noticed.

Didn't comment.

He parked at the pullout and shut off the engine. The river sounded the same as it always had.

Steady.

Emily stepped out, walked closer to the water, and then—deliberately—sat on a smooth rock and pulled off her shoes and socks. She lined them up together before standing again.

The cold hit immediately when she stepped in. Sharp. Bracing.

Blake stayed on the bank for a moment, watching her like he was giving her space to choose it. Then he stepped closer, still barefoot, stopping just short of the water.

"They named her," Emily said.

"I know," he said.

"They still didn't say how."

"No."

The river moved around her ankles, indifferent.

"When does that come?" she asked.

Blake was quiet for a moment. Then, "When someone has to answer for it."

Emily shifted her footing and leaned into him then—on purpose. Not because she slipped.

Blake's hand came to her wrist immediately. Steady. Familiar.

She breathed there for a moment, letting the cold and the contact do their work.

After a while, Emily stepped back out of the water. She dried her feet on the hem of her jeans, slid her socks and shoes back on, and tied them properly.

"I should check on Zoe," she said.

Blake nodded. "I'll take you."

On the drive back, he didn't turn the radio on. He didn't fill the space. One hand stayed loose on the wheel, the other resting close enough that she could feel its presence without needing to touch it.

At Zoe's house, he pulled up to the curb and shut off the engine.

"I should go," Emily said. "Before Zoe starts narrating my disappearance."

He smiled. "She's thorough."

Emily hesitated, then leaned across the seat and pressed a quick kiss to his cheek.

It surprised both of them.

He stilled for half a second—then smiled, softer.

"Text me," he said.

"I will."

Zoe opened the door before Emily reached it.

"I was about to start a missing-person narrative," Zoe said.

Emily smiled faintly. Zoe always framed worry like a joke. It made it easier to carry.

"I stopped at the river," Emily added.

Zoe studied her for a second. "Okay," she said. "That tracks."

Emily went inside.

Behind her, Blake's truck pulled away, unhurried.

The name had been spoken.

The ground beneath it was still shifting.

But Emily felt steady enough now to stand in it—shoes on, feet planted, not alone.

CHAPTER THIRTY ONE

Moving Water

By the fourth day, the quiet had started to feel intentional.

Not peaceful—deliberate. Like something was being held in place because no one wanted to name it yet.

Emily tried staying inside. Tried sitting at the table while Kate drew measurements that never seemed to end. Tried reading without absorbing a single sentence. By late afternoon, the air in the house felt thick, unmoving.

She grabbed her keys and told her mom she was going for a drive.

Her mom nodded. "Okay."

No questions. No warnings. Just trust—or maybe understanding.

Emily took the right fork in the road. Away from the basin. Toward the river.

The pullout was already occupied.

Blake's pickup sat angled near the trees, dust settled into the wheel wells like it hadn't just arrived. Emily slowed without thinking. She didn't ask herself why he was there.

She parked a few spaces down.

The river ran steady below them, unchanged. No tape. No trucks. No people pretending to be official. Just water doing what it had always done.

Emily shut off her engine and got out.

Blake was leaning against the side of his truck, watching the water. He turned when he heard her door close. No surprise crossed his face—just recognition.

"You're going to step on something awful," she said wryly.

He glanced down at her feet, then back up at her, a familiar, lopsided grin tugging at his mouth.

"Worth it," he said.

She shook her head. "That's not how risk assessment works."

He shrugged. "Hasn't killed me yet."

She didn't argue. She slipped her shoes off and set them side by side at the edge of the bank, the ground cool and soft beneath her feet.

She didn't ask how he knew she'd come here.

Blake had always known which way she turned when the noise got loud.

"You going in?" he asked.

Emily nodded.

They stepped into the river together.

The cold hit fast, sharp enough to steal her breath before settling into something numbing and clean. Emily closed her eyes for a second and let it run over her ankles, her calves, the ache grounding her in her body again.

Beside her, Blake stood solid, the current breaking around him. When she shifted on the uneven stones, she leaned into him—just slightly.

Not falling.

Choosing.

He adjusted without comment, steadying her with his shoulder, his stance widening like it was instinct.

They stood like that, feet in the water, saying nothing.

The river moved past them, indifferent to waiting, to procedures, to names not yet spoken.

When Emily stepped back, she crouched and picked up her shoes, tucking them under her arm instead of putting them on. Her feet were pink and numb, alive in a way that made her feel real again.

"You hungry?" Blake asked.

She nodded. "Yeah."

"DQ's open," he said. "Burgers, not cones."

"Good," she said. "I need something solid."

They walked back up the bank together. Emily didn't rush to put her shoes on. The gravel pressed into her feet, sharp and honest.

They didn't leave at the same time.

Emily pulled onto the road first.

A mile later, Blake's pickup eased up beside her at the stop sign, idling close enough that she could see him through the open window.

"DQ," he said. Not a question.

"Yeah."

"I'll meet you there."

She nodded, then drove on.

The river stayed behind her, still moving, still doing its quiet work.

But something else had shifted.

Not loudly. Not all at once.

Just enough to matter.

CHAPTER THIRTY TWO

After the Name

E mily heard the name on the radio.

It came between a farm report and an update on the dam repairs, the announcer's voice shifting into the careful, neutral cadence reserved for things that had been confirmed but not yet explained.

"Authorities say the remains recovered near the Jennings property belong to Clara Jennings, who went missing in 1965, the year the reservoir was first filled. Officials emphasize that the investigation is ongoing and that no determination has been made regarding the circumstances of her death."

Emily stood at the kitchen counter, one hand resting against the edge, the kettle humming softly behind her. She didn't move until the segment ended. The name didn't arrive as news so much as completion—something long unfinished finally given a sentence of its own.

Clara Jennings.

The paper carried it the next morning. A short article on the inside pages. No photograph. No speculation. Just the known dates, the known absence, and the confirmation that the question the town had learned to live with finally had an answer, if not an explanation.

By the time the county posted its statement later that day, the name already felt settled into place.

In town, people spoke it with a kind of cautious relief.

"So it really was Clara Jennings," an older man said near the end of the grocery aisle, leaning on his cart.

His companion nodded. "I always wondered what became of her."

Emily heard versions of the exchange throughout the week, always from people old enough to remember when the reservoir went in the first time. People whose memories had carried Clara as a loose end for most of their lives.

What she did *not* hear was grief.

No one cried. No one gathered. Clara had been missing for sixty years. Whatever mourning there had been belonged to another time, one that had already thinned and passed on. This was not loss arriving—it was uncertainty ending.

This was clarification.

Emily walked past the high school that afternoon. The building was closed for summer, classrooms dark, the glass case near the front doors still holding orientation flyers taped there the week before. School hadn't started yet. There were no routines to disrupt.

Outside the hardware store, her grandfather stood beside his truck, keys in hand. Grandpa looked up when she approached, his expression thoughtful rather than surprised.

"They finally said it out loud," he said.

"Yes," Emily replied.

He nodded once. "I figured they would, eventually."

She waited.

"I never knew what happened to her," he said after a moment. "Not for sure. Just that she was gone."

He looked past Emily toward the street, as if measuring distance. "For a long time, I thought maybe she'd come back after the reservoir was filled. Like somehow... that would resolve it."

Emily didn't respond. There was nothing to correct.

The hardware store door opened behind him. Martha stepped out with a folded receipt in her hand. When she saw Emily, her face softened in a way that didn't draw attention but did change something.

"There you are," she said, as if Emily had been expected.

Emily smiled back. "Hi, Grandma."

Martha reached out and touched Emily's arm briefly—just long enough to anchor her—before turning to Grandpa.

"You ready?" she asked.

Grandpa nodded. He opened the passenger door for her and waited until she was settled before closing it, then walked around to the driver's side.

Martha glanced back once through the open window. "We'll be home later," she said. "You eating with us?"

Emily nodded. "Probably."

"Good," Martha said. "Text me if you change your mind."

The truck pulled away, her grandparents framed together through the windshield—easy, familiar, unchanged.

By the end of the week, Clara had taken on a shape the town could hold.

An old yearbook photo appeared on the bulletin board outside the library, pinned slightly crooked. Someone left flowers beneath it a day later—simple, unmarked. People paused, looked, and moved on.

"She was a swimmer," an elderly woman said to the man beside her as Emily passed. "Good, too. I remember watching her at the meets."

He nodded. "Strong girl. Confident in the water."

Emily noted it without knowing why.

On Friday afternoon, a new notice appeared on the community board.

MEMORIAL FOR CLARA JENNINGS
SATURDAY — 3:00 PM

No location yet. Just a time.

Emily stood there longer than necessary. Clara's name had finally been set down, but it hadn't finished its work. It had only shifted from question to presence—something the town would now have to remember deliberately.

Beyond town, the reservoir remained held in place, the dam still under repair, the Jennings site still cordoned off. Nothing was moving yet.

Some things, Emily understood, waited until they were told they could.

CHAPTER THIRTY THREE

Rising Water

In the present, the reservoir wasn't moving.

That was the phrase people used when they talked about it—*moving*—as if water had intention, as if it could be coaxed into patience. The level was being held while the dam was repaired and the Jennings site remained under investigation, measured and marked and watched.

Still, Emily found herself thinking about rising.

Not the controlled rise of charts and gauges, but the other kind—the one people talked about when they were remembering instead of explaining. The kind that had a year attached to it the way some storms did.

1965.

She started noticing how often it came up now that Clara's name had been said out loud again.

At the library, an elderly man stood longer than necessary in front of a laminated display mounted near the local history shelves. It showed a timeline of the reservoir project, neat blocks of text interrupted by grainy photographs. He traced the years with one finger, stopping at the circled date.

"At the end," he said, not looking at her, "it wasn't a flood. People forget that."

Emily paused beside him. "What was it, then?"

He glanced up, surprised, then shrugged. "A plan. That's what made it harder. You could see it coming."

Emily carried that with her when she left.

That afternoon, she drove out to her grandparents' house. The road was familiar enough that she barely noticed the turns, the hills rising and falling the way they always had. Grandma's car was already in the driveway when Emily pulled in.

Grandma opened the door before Emily had a chance to knock.

"There you are," she said, pulling Emily into a quick hug. "Come in."

The house smelled like coffee and lemon cleaner. Grandpa sat at the kitchen table with the newspaper folded beside his plate, his glasses perched low on his nose.

"They've got it held steady for now," Grandpa said, nodding toward the muted television in the corner as Emily took a seat.

"That's what they're saying," Emily replied.

"It wasn't like that the first time," Grandpa said.

Grandma set a mug in front of Emily and leaned against the counter. "They told people ahead of time," she said. "Letters. Meetings. Maps. They didn't pretend it was a surprise."

"They had markers out," Grandpa added. "Painted lines. Stakes in the ground. You could stand there and see where the water was supposed to stop."

Emily pictured it—people walking their own land with measuring tapes and notebooks, trying to make sense of a future already scheduled.

"People think it came all at once," Grandma said. "But it didn't."

Emily waited.

"The town wasn't empty yet," Grandpa said. "Most people were still there for graduation. They were just already packed up to leave that night, as soon as it was over."

Grandma nodded. "Cars loaded. Boxes stacked by the doors."

"The water was already moving by then," Grandpa added. "Not fast. Just enough that you could see it covering things you recognized. Fence posts. Corners of fields. The kind of landmarks you didn't think about until they weren't where they were supposed to be."

Grandma was quiet for a moment. "It wasn't dramatic," she said. "That's what people get wrong. You could just tell it wasn't stopping."

Emily imagined the gym—folding chairs lined in rows, borrowed flowers tied with ribbon, the smell of floor wax and dust. Outside, familiar ground slowly losing its edges.

"Was it strange?" she asked.

Grandpa considered that. "Not strange," he said. "Measured. Everything about it was measured."

"And that was the strangest part," Grandma said.

They talked a little longer, drifting back to ordinary things—how long the repairs were expected to take, who had stopped by earlier that day, whether the memorial notice had gone up yet. Nothing was forced. Nothing circled back on itself.

When Emily stood to leave, Grandma followed her to the door.

"You drive careful," Grandma said, her hand warm on Emily's arm.

"I will."

"Come by Grandpaorrow if you want," Grandma added. "We'll be around."

Outside, the evening air had cooled. Emily paused on the porch long enough to hear the low murmur of the television inside, Grandpa's voice responding to something Grandma had said. Ordinary sounds. Intact.

She drove home with the windows down.

Later, in her own room, Emily lay awake listening to the familiar sounds of her parents' house settling. Kate's door creaked softly down the hall. A car passed on the road outside, tires crunching briefly on gravel.

She thought of the bench above town. The gym lit against the dark. The way the water had risen then—not violently, not suddenly, but with the certainty of something already decided.

Graduation night hadn't been a storm.

It had been a schedule.

Sixty years later, the lake was still doing what it had been told to do—rising when scheduled, stopping where it was meant to.

Emily closed her eyes and let the image settle.

The rising had begun long before anyone was ready to name it.

CHAPTER THIRTY FOUR

Swim Team

Emily heard about the swim team the way she heard about most things lately—incidentally.

It came up in passing, folded into conversations that weren't meant to go anywhere. Names resurfaced. Years were mentioned. Nothing lingered long enough to feel deliberate.

At the library, the bulletin board near the local history shelves had filled in around the memorial notice. Someone had pinned up an old yearbook photo, the edges curled slightly. Two older women stood in front of it, their shoulders nearly touching.

"That's Clara," one of them said.

The other woman nodded. "I remember."

They didn't look sad. They didn't look curious. Just certain.

"She swam," the first woman said. "Same team as Martha."

Emily slowed near the end of the aisle, pretending to read the spines of books she already knew.

"She was fast," the second woman said.

"Consistently," the first woman replied.

There was a pause, the natural kind that comes when a memory has reached its end.

"Martha was faster," the second woman added, without emphasis. "In freestyle."

"That's true," the first woman said. "Always had a finish."

They moved on then, conversation shifting easily to someone else's name, someone else's story. Emily stepped closer to the board and read the memorial notice, as if that had been her intention all along.

At home, her mother was sorting mail at the counter. Kate sat at the table with her sketchbook open, pencil moving steadily across the page.

"They confirmed it again today," her mother said. "That Clara was found in the cellar."

Emily nodded. "That's where the email said."

Her mother folded an envelope and set it aside. "I keep forgetting how long she's been missing," she said. "It's strange, having a name come back like that."

Kate pushed her sketchbook toward Emily. "Look."

Emily leaned in.

Kate had drawn the valley carefully—the bench rising above town, the house placed where the slope dropped away, the cellar suggested by darker shading at the foundation. The lake sat unfinished below it, its edge left light, open.

"I used the maps," Kate said, matter-of-fact. "And the old photos. They line up."

Emily nodded and slid the sketchbook back gently.

That evening, she stopped by her grandparents' house.

Grandma was at the counter, rinsing a mug. Grandpa sat at the table, the television turned low.

"There you are," Grandma said, smiling. "Sit."

Emily did.

After a few minutes, she said, "People have been talking about the swim team."

Grandma nodded. "They always do, once they start remembering."

"They mention Clara," Emily said. "And you."

Grandma dried her hands and folded the towel. "We were on the same team," she said. "For a while."

"They say she was good."

"She was," Grandma said easily. "Fast. Competitive."

"And you?" Emily asked.

Grandma met her eyes. "I trained more," she said. "That's usually how it goes."

Grandpa smiled. "Your grandma didn't like being second."

Grandma gave him a look. "Nobody does."

Emily smiled despite herself.

They didn't stay on the subject. They didn't need to. The conversation drifted to the memorial, to who might attend, to whether the weather would hold.

When Emily stood to leave, Grandma walked her to the door.

"People remember different parts of the same thing," Grandma said, her hand resting briefly on Emily's arm. "That's not the same as knowing it."

"I know," Emily said.

Driving home, Emily didn't try to make sense of what she'd heard.

She let it sit the way the town seemed to be letting it sit—facts resurfacing, names returning to use, nothing yet asking to be arranged into meaning.

Some stories didn't ask to be solved.

They only asked to be remembered.

CHAPTER THIRTY FIVE

Records

The county's statement came midweek.

It was brief and narrowly framed, delivered through the same channels as the earlier updates. It addressed only what investigators could responsibly say after so much time.

Clara Jennings' death was determined not to have been accidental. It was not the result of drowning. Beyond that, the statement explained, the available evidence, after sixty years underwater, did not allow for further conclusions.

Emily heard it once on the radio and read it again later in the paper. The language was careful, deliberate, bounded by what sixty years underwater had erased.

At the library, people lingered longer than usual near the local history shelves.

Old yearbooks were pulled down and returned. Graduation programs from the sixties lay open on the table, pages held flat by hands that had learned where to be gentle. It wasn't curiosity so much as recognition—faces and names revisited now that Clara's had returned to use.

Emily was looking through the 1965 graduation program when Blake stepped closer. He leaned in, close enough that she could smell his coffee, and tapped a name near the middle of the page.

"My grandpa," he said quietly. "Same class."

Emily followed his finger. "He graduated with my grandparents."

Blake nodded. "Yeah. He talks about that year like it was the last one before everything started changing."

Zoe hovered a few steps away, scanning another page. "Before people realized they couldn't wait things out," she said.

Emily closed the program and slid it back onto the stack.

Later that evening, she was home when her mother mentioned the statement again while clearing the table.

"They were careful," her mother said. "They said what they could and stopped there."

Emily nodded.

Kate sat nearby with her sketchbook open, erasing and redrawing the same line along the edge of the page.

"So they know how she died," Kate said, not looking up.

"They know enough to say it wasn't an accident," their mother replied. "That's all."

Emily listened without comment.

Some things, once defined, didn't need revisiting.

They simply took their place—on a page, in a memory, in the space between what could be known and what would remain carried.

CHAPTER THIRTY SIX

Pressure

The announcement came early enough that it caught people in the middle of their mornings.

Emily heard it from the kitchen while her mother packed lunches, the radio voice steady and practiced, as if the words had been read and reread before being released.

Repairs to the dam had been completed.
The reservoir would begin refilling at a controlled rate the following week.

Her mother paused with a piece of foil halfway over a container.

"So that's it," she said.

Emily waited.

"They must be confident in the repairs," her mother added, already turning back to the counter. "They wouldn't start again otherwise."

The radio moved on to weather, then traffic. Emily poured her coffee and stood there longer than she meant to, listening for the announcement to repeat. It didn't.

At school, the water came back into conversation the way it always did when something long paused decided to resume.

Not urgently. Not dramatically. Just enough to alter the rhythm of things.

Someone mentioned it at the lockers. Someone else said they'd heard the memorial was set for Saturday. A teacher paused mid-sentence when the PA crackled and then continued as if nothing had happened.

Zoe slid into the seat beside Emily in English, her notebook still closed.

"My mom texted me the flyer," she said quietly. "Like I hadn't already seen it."

Emily nodded. "Everyone's mom texted everyone."

"They said they're starting next week," Zoe added. "After the memorial."

"Yes."

Zoe tapped her pen against the desk. "It feels...early."

Emily thought of the radio voice. The measured phrasing. "It feels like paperwork."

Zoe grimaced. "That's worse."

Between classes, Blake fell into step beside Emily, close enough that he didn't have to raise his voice.

"My grandpa heard the announcement," he said. "He said the wording was almost the same as the one they made before graduation in sixty-five."

"What did he remember about it?" Emily asked.

"That people listened," Blake said. "More than they admitted. Because once they set a date, there wasn't anything left to argue about."

Emily nodded. That felt familiar.

After school, Emily drove home and found Kate on the floor with her sketchbook open, papers spread around her like she'd been trying to decide which one mattered.

"They're going to start filling it again," Kate said, without looking up.

"I know."

Kate hesitated, then looked up. "Can we go up there?"

Emily didn't need to ask where.

"Sure," she said. "Get your jacket."

The road out of town curved gently, climbing just enough that the air shifted when Emily rolled down the window. The overlook lot was fuller than she expected—not crowded, just occupied. Cars parked at careful angles. People standing in small groups or alone, hands in pockets, bodies angled toward the view.

Evansville lay exposed below them.

Foundations. Streets that ended abruptly. The outlines of buildings no one would ever walk into again. The remains were pale against the darker earth, a town reduced to shape and suggestion.

Kate climbed onto the low wall and opened her sketchbook.

"They'll be underwater soon," she said.

"Yes."

Kate began to draw anyway.

Emily stood beside her, watching how people chose their places. Some stood close to the edge. Others kept back, as if distance might preserve something. A woman set a small bundle of flowers near a stone marker and stepped away without ceremony.

Emily understood now what the flyer had meant—*before it gets too far along*. While there was still something to see.

On the drive home, Kate closed her sketchbook without showing Emily the page.

That evening, Emily stopped by her grandparents' house.

Grandma was at the counter folding the memorial flyer along its creases, smoothing it flat again. Grandpa sat at the table reading the same paper upside down.

"They picked Saturday," Grandpa said.

"Before they start again," Grandma added.

Emily nodded. "That makes sense."

Grandma looked at her then. Not searching. Just attentive. "You took Kate up there."

"Yes."

"That was a good idea," Grandma said.

They talked for a few minutes—about the weather, about who might attend, about whether the road would be busy that day. Nothing heavy. Nothing forced.

At home, Emily lay awake listening to the house settle. Her parents' voices drifted faintly from the living room. Kate's door creaked down the hall.

The pressure wasn't fear. It wasn't memory.

It was timing.

A week between stillness and movement.

A Saturday set aside before erasure resumed.

Emily understood that once the water began to rise again, it wouldn't pause for anyone who wasn't ready.

It would only continue.

And whatever was going to be said would need to be said before that.

<h1>CHAPTER THIRTY SEVEN</h1>

Narrowing

Grandma had started correcting people.

Not directly. Not in a way that drew attention. Just small adjustments, offered once and then released, as if accuracy were a habit rather than a defense.

Emily noticed it first at the kitchen table.

They were talking about the memorial—who might attend, how early people would arrive, whether the road to the overlook would hold the traffic.

"I remember she went into the water that night," Grandpa said, folding the flyer again. "After graduation. She was upset."

Grandma nodded. "She was angry," she said. "And crying."

Grandpa looked up at her. "Yes."

"She said she was going back to her room," Grandma added, her voice even. "That's what she told you."

Grandpa's mouth tightened briefly. "That's what she said."

The distinction settled there. Not argued. Not explained.

Later, as Grandma and Emily folded laundry together, a neighbor's voice carried in through the open window.

"They keep saying it all happened so fast," the woman said. "Like no one had time to think."

Grandma smoothed a towel carefully. "There was time," she said, not raising her voice. "Just not the kind people like to imagine."

Emily watched her hands.

"They talk like the water caused it," Grandma went on. "But the water was already there."

Emily nodded. That, at least, was true.

As the afternoon wore on, Grandma and Grandpa were both in the kitchen. Grandpa sat at the table with the paper open, reading slowly. Grandma moved between the counter and the stove, methodical.

"They've got a sign-up sheet going around," Grandpa said. "For Saturday."

Grandma nodded. "I put my name down."

"For what?" Emily asked.

"Brownies," Grandma said. "Something simple."

Grandpa smiled faintly. "People eat when they don't know what else to do."

No one disagreed.

Later, Grandma and Emily drove together to pick up groceries. The road was familiar, the light steady.

"They keep getting the order wrong," Grandma said as they waited at a stoplight. "They talk like one thing led straight to another."

Emily glanced at her. "But it didn't."

"No," Grandma said. "There were choices. And then there was water."

The light changed. Grandma drove on.

At the store, they moved through the aisles without hurry. Grandma compared labels, replaced one box with another nearly identical.

"They'll want to talk afterward," she said as they stood in line. "They always do."

Emily nodded.

"You and Kate don't have to stay," Grandma added. "You can leave when you're ready."

"Are you going to?" Emily asked.

Grandma's hands tightened briefly on the cart handle. "Yes."

They unloaded the groceries back at the house in silence.

Before Emily left, Grandma paused at the door, her hand resting against the frame.

"You've been patient," she said.

Emily met her eyes. "With what?"

Grandma considered her for a moment. "With people smoothing things out," she said. "So they fit better than they did."

Emily didn't argue.

That night, lying awake, Emily replayed the words Grandma had chosen.

Angry.

Crying.

Said she was going back to her room.

There was time.

The water was already there.

None of it contradicted what Grandpa remembered.

But it changed the shape of the story—pared it down to what could not be moved or softened.

Emily understood then that Grandma wasn't correcting people to control the story.

She was clearing space.

So that when the truth finally arrived, it wouldn't have to fight its way through comfort.

CHAPTER THIRTY EIGHT

What People Knew

Emily started noticing how often Clara's name came up when no one meant to talk about her.

At first it was small things. A pause in conversation that lasted a beat too long. A name mentioned and then quickly corrected to something else. The way people lowered their voices without realizing they'd done it.

At the post office, two women stood near the bulletin board longer than necessary, one pointing at the memorial flyer, the other nodding without really looking.

"I still can't believe it took this long," the first woman said.

"Well," the second replied, folding her arms, "people didn't want to look too close back then."

Emily pretended to read the notices beneath the flyer while she waited for her mail.

"They keep saying it was sudden," the first woman went on. "Like she just went out and—"

She made a vague motion with her hand.

"She was upset," the woman added. "Everyone knew that."

Emily slid an envelope from her box and held it loosely, not opening it.

"That fight was right outside the gym," the second woman said. "People saw it. Heard it."

"Yeah, but once Tom turned and went back inside," the first said, "everyone else did too."

Emily's fingers tightened around the envelope.

They didn't say Tom's name again. They didn't need to.

Later, at school, Zoe leaned over during study hall, lowering her voice even though no one was listening.

"My aunt says it wasn't like people think," she said.

Emily kept writing.

"What do you mean?" she asked carefully.

Zoe shrugged. "Just that someone followed her. Not like—" she waved a hand, vague. "Not a guy. Another girl."

Emily stopped her pen.

"That's not what people usually say," she said.

Zoe tilted her head. "Yeah, well. My aunt's lived here forever. She says there were things people knew and just...didn't say."

Emily closed her notebook.

"Who?" she asked.

Zoe hesitated, then shook her head. "She didn't say names."

That afternoon, Emily ducked into the hardware store with her mother, claiming she needed a notebook for school. She wandered down an aisle she didn't need, stopping short when two women turned the corner ahead of her.

"I still don't understand why Martha didn't go after her," one of them said.

Emily froze, half-hidden by a rack of lightbulbs.

The other woman sighed. "She probably did."

"No, I mean—right away," the first woman said. "Before it got out of hand."

They stopped near the paint samples, voices lowered but not hushed.

"If anyone could've talked Clara down, it was Martha," the second woman said. "Everyone knew that."

Emily's chest tightened.

"Clara could get spun up," the first woman went on. "Emotional. Impulsive. Always chasing the feeling of something."

"But Martha was steady," the second said. "She was the one Clara listened to. The one who could slow her down."

Emily stared at the shelf in front of her without seeing it.

"She'd done it before," the first woman said. "More than once. Remember senior year, when Clara was talking about leaving early? Martha sat with her all night."

The second woman nodded. "That's what I mean. If Martha was there—"

The sentence trailed off.

Emily set the box she was holding back on the shelf with care and walked away before either woman noticed her.

That night, lying in bed, Emily replayed the fragments.

Everyone knew she was upset.

The fight was public.

Martha was steady.

Martha was the one Clara listened to.

None of it accused anyone.

But all of it pointed in the same direction.

By the time sleep finally came, Emily understood what her mind had been circling all day:

There was only one person in her world who seemed clear on what had actually happened.

And she hadn't told anyone yet.

CHAPTER THIRTY NINE

The Truth

Emily went to her grandparents' house because something no longer fit.

It wasn't what people were saying. It was what Grandma knew.

Not the public facts—graduation night, the water rising, Clara going into the lake. Those had been repeated enough to sound smooth, rehearsed.

It was the details.

Angry.

Crying.

Said she was going back to her room.

Those weren't the kinds of things people remembered cleanly after sixty years. They were the kinds of things you knew because you had been there.

Emily pulled into the driveway and sat for a moment before getting out, her hands tight on the steering wheel.

Inside, Grandpa was in the living room with the television on low.

"Hey, kiddo," he said. "Your grandma made soup."

"I'm okay," Emily said. Her voice sounded strange to her own ears.

Grandma stood at the counter, one hand braced against it, the other wrapped around a mug she wasn't drinking from.

"Sit," she said.

Emily sat. The memorial flyer lay folded between them.

For a long moment, Grandma didn't speak.

Emily waited. Her hand drifted to the loose strands at the base of her neck, absently trying to weave them back into her.

Grandma noticed it too. She pulled the chair back with her foot and sat down heavily.

"I didn't mean for it to happen," she said.

Her voice broke immediately.

Emily's chest tightened.

Grandma swallowed hard, then a sob tore out of her — sharp, sudden, uncontrollable. She bent forward, one hand slapping the table, the other covering her mouth as she fought to breathe.

Emily made a small, involuntary sound and half-rose from her chair, then stopped herself.

"Don't," Grandma said hoarsely, lifting one hand. "Just—just let me get it out."

Emily sank back down, heart pounding.

Grandma wiped her face with shaking hands.

"But I did it," she said. "I did."

Emily's stomach dropped.

"I killed Clara," Grandma said.

Emily flinched, the words hitting her like a physical blow.

"No," Emily said automatically, even as her mind raced to catch up. "Grandma—"

Grandma shook her head, tears streaming.

"I did," she said. "I need you to hear me say it."

Emily's hands clenched in her lap.

Grandma stared down at the table.

"You've been trying to make sense of the order," she said. "You keep circling it. That's why you came."

Emily swallowed. "You know things you shouldn't know."

Grandma nodded, a broken sound leaving her throat.

"Because I was there," she said.

Emily's pulse roared in her ears.

"It was graduation night," Grandma said, words coming unevenly. "The gym was up on the bench. The water hadn't reached it yet, but it was already rising below town."

Emily shook her head slowly. "People say it all happened at once."

"They're wrong," Grandma said sharply, then immediately dissolved again. "It never happens all at once."

She dragged a hand down her face.

"Clara and your grandpa argued by the gym doors," Grandma said. "People everywhere. Music still playing."

Emily's chest tightened. "You saw them?"

"Yes." Grandma pressed her palm to the table. "She told him she was leaving. That she wanted him to come with her."

Emily closed her eyes.

"He told her he couldn't," Grandma said. "He had obligations. The farm. His family. A life he couldn't walk away from."

Emily whispered, "He always talks about that summer like it was already decided."

Grandma nodded miserably.

"She got angry," she said. "She cried. She yelled. And then she walked straight into the water while she was still yelling at him."

Emily's breath hitched. "Right there?"

"Yes," Grandma said. "She waded in while he could still hear her."

Emily pressed both palms flat to the table, grounding herself.

"She said if he wouldn't come," Grandma continued, "she was going to swim back down to her room and stay there."

Emily's voice shook. "And he thought she was bluffing."

"Yes," Grandma said. "He turned back toward the gym."

Emily swallowed hard. "And you?"

"I followed her," Grandma said, voice cracking. "Because I was crying too. Because I was angry. Because I loved him."

Emily sucked in a sharp breath.

"You loved Grandpa," she said.

"Yes," Grandma said. "And I hated myself for it."

Emily felt something twist painfully in her chest.

"By the time I reached her, it was dark," Grandma said. "The water was cold. She was standing in it, crying. Not drowning. Not even close."

Emily shook her head. "She was a swimmer."

"Yes," Grandma said. "She was strong. Fast. She wasn't afraid of the water."

Her hands curled into fists.

"She turned on me," Grandma said. "Said I didn't get to stop her. Said I didn't get to protect him from her choices."

Emily whispered, "What did you say?"

"I begged her," Grandma said, sobbing again. "I begged her to stop."

Emily's eyes burned.

"She laughed," Grandma went on. "She said he'd regret it. That he'd spend his whole life wishing he'd gone."

Emily's voice came out raw. "That's cruel."

"Yes," Grandma said. "And I lost myself."

She stared at the table, breathing hard.

"There was a rock," she whispered.

Emily froze. "Grandma..."

"I picked it up," Grandma said. "I don't know why. I don't."

Emily covered her mouth, tears spilling.

"She turned toward me," Grandma said, voice breaking completely now. "And I swung."

Emily let out a broken sound.

"She went still," Grandma sobbed. "Just—just like that."

Emily stood abruptly, pacing a step, then stopping herself.

"No," Emily whispered, the word barely making it out.

"I shook her," Grandma said. "I called her name. I shook her and begged her to wake up."

Emily pressed her fists to her eyes.

"And when I knew," Grandma said, "when I knew she wasn't coming back—I couldn't leave her there."

Emily whispered, "So you swam her."

"Yes," Grandma said. "Down."

Emily felt dizzy. "The cellar."

"Yes," Grandma said. "I swam her to it. I held her the whole way."

Emily slid back into her chair, trembling.

"I laid her down," Grandma said. "I tried to move her hair out of her face, but it kept floating up around her head, as out of control as I felt in that moment."

Emily sobbed quietly.

"She was my best friend," Grandma said.

They sat in silence for a long time.

Eventually, Grandma spoke again, voice hoarse.

"The rain started while I was still out there," she said. "By the time I climbed back up, everyone was soaked. Everyone was moving. No one noticed."

Emily wiped her face. "Grandpa never knew."

"No," Grandma said. "But he knew I knew more than I should."

Emily nodded slowly.

"The email," she said.

"You sent it," Grandma said.

Emily nodded. "I didn't know what else to do."

"I didn't stop you," Grandma said. "Because I couldn't keep it buried anymore." She hesitated and bit her bottom lip, looked up at Emily briefly, then dropped her eyes to her hands. "You saw her," she whispered. "In the cellar."

Emily couldn't trust herself to speak around the lump in her throat. She nodded slowly in response and then squeezed her eyes shut like it would erase the memory she carried burned into her brain.

They sat together, tears still falling, neither speaking.

After a long while, Emily stood and walked around the table.

She hesitated, then wrapped her arms around her grandmother.

Grandma stiffened, then let herself lean into it, sobbing once more before pulling back.

She wiped her face. Took a breath. Another.

They walked toward the door together.

In the living room, Grandpa looked up.

"Saturday's bringing a lot back," he said quietly.

Emily nodded. "Yeah."

"You drive safe."

"I will."

On the porch, Grandma held Emily's arm.

"You don't decide tonight," Grandma said. "But you need to understand this."

Emily looked at her.

"You can't un-know it," Grandma said. "And you can't save everyone."

Emily swallowed. "I know."

Grandma nodded and opened the door.

The truth hadn't come like lightning.

It had come like water.

Already there.

CHAPTER FORTY

Holding

Emily drove home with the radio off.

The rain-wet road was muddy, gravel plinking against the underside of the pickup, the valley behind her waiting—exposed for a few more days before the water came back and smoothed it over like nothing had ever happened.

She kept both hands on the wheel like she could keep herself in place by force.

When she pulled into her parents' driveway, the porch light was on even though it wasn't fully dark yet. The house looked the same as it had that morning. Warm windows. Familiar shapes. The life she'd had before she knew what she knew.

Inside, her mother's voice drifted from the kitchen.

"Hey—Emily?"

Emily closed the door softly behind her.

"In here," her mother called.

Kate's laugh followed—quick and bright—before she bent back over her sketchbook.

Emily stepped into the kitchen.

Her mother stood at the counter with a cutting board, a row of carrots lined neatly beside her knife. She glanced up, took in Emily's face, and didn't say what she saw.

Kate sat at the table with her sketchbook open, pencil moving in small, careful strokes.

"You were at Grandma and Grandpa's?" her mother asked.

Emily nodded. She could feel the nod happen like someone else did it.

"How are they?" her mother asked.

Emily opened her mouth and nothing came out.

Kate looked up. Her eyes flicked over Emily's face, then down again, pencil pausing.

Her mother set the knife down slowly.

"Emily," she said, gentle. "Are you okay?"

Emily forced a breath through her nose. "I'm fine."

It wasn't a lie. Not exactly. Fine was just a word people used when they didn't know what shape the truth could take.

Her mother studied her a moment longer, then nodded once, letting it go the way she always did when Emily asked her to.

"Dinner's almost ready," she said.

Kate's pencil started moving again.

Emily went to her room and shut the door.

She stood there with her hand still on the knob.

On the other side of the wall, the house continued. Cabinet doors. Water running. Kate's chair scraping lightly when she shifted.

Emily sat on the edge of her bed and pressed her palms to her eyes until the pressure turned into something close to pain.

She saw Grandma's hands trembling.

She heard it again—the sound Grandma made before she could stop it.

I killed Clara.

The words didn't echo like a movie line. They sat heavy and ordinary, like a stone dropped into a pocket you couldn't take off.

Emily lay back and stared at the ceiling until the light outside her window went from gray to darker gray.

At dinner, her father talked about a fence line that needed repairing before the weather turned. Her mother asked Kate about an art assignment. Kate answered, animated, describing paper size and shading, the way she got when she was excited about something she could control.

Emily ate because she was supposed to.

Every so often, her mother glanced at her, and Emily kept her face neutral and her chewing steady.

"This weekend's the memorial," her father said at one point, like he was reminding himself as much as anyone else.

Emily's fork paused halfway to her mouth.

Her mother nodded. "We should leave early."

Kate's eyes lifted. "Are we going?"

Her father shrugged. "If you want to."

"I want to see it," Kate said. "Before they fill it."

Emily felt her throat tighten.

Her mother looked at Emily. "Do you want to go?"

Emily kept her fork moving. "Sure."

It came out flat. Her mother didn't comment.

After dinner, Kate followed Emily down the hall.

"Hey," she said, hovering in Emily's doorway.

Emily turned.

Kate held her sketchbook against her chest.

"You're being weird," Kate said.

Emily almost laughed. It would have sounded wrong.

"I'm tired," Emily said.

Kate studied her. "Did Grandma say something?"

Emily's heartbeat jumped.

"No," she said too quickly, and felt it—the speed of it, the way it gave her away.

Kate's eyes narrowed.

"Okay," Kate said slowly. "Then why do you look like you saw something you weren't supposed to see?"

Emily held her sister's gaze.

Kate wasn't accusing. She was noticing. The way she always did, even when she pretended not to.

Emily forced a breath.

"Because everyone keeps talking," she said carefully. "Like the memorial fixes things."

Kate frowned. "Doesn't it?"

Emily looked away.

"It...closes something," she said, choosing her words the way Grandma had.

Kate's frown deepened, like she didn't like answers that could fold into themselves.

She hugged the sketchbook tighter.

"You've been quiet since you got back," Kate said.

Emily hesitated.

"I guess," she said.

Kate nodded, but she didn't look satisfied. She turned and walked back down the hall, the floor creaking softly under her steps.

Emily shut her door and leaned her forehead against it.

She understood something then, sharp and immediate:

This was what Grandma had been doing for sixty years.

Living inside ordinary days with an extraordinary truth pressed up against them.

Sleep came in pieces.

Emily woke more than once with her heart racing, the house quiet, the dark outside her window thick and unmoving.

When she drifted off again, she dreamed of water that didn't rush.

Water that rose in a straight line, patient and unstoppable.

In the morning, school still existed.

The hallway smelled like wet coats and floor cleaner. Lockers banged. Someone laughed too loudly. The world went on like the truth was none of its business.

Emily sat through first period with her notebook open, her pen moving without meaning.

In history class, Mr. Tolland put a map on the board and talked about infrastructure projects—dams and reservoirs, the way towns got moved or erased.

He said the word *relocated* like it was neutral.

Emily stared at the map until her vision blurred.

Beside her, Zoe leaned over and whispered, "My mom says the county got calls from three different true-crime podcasts."

Emily blinked. "What?"

Zoe rolled her eyes. "You know. People are gross. They want a story."

Emily kept her face still. "It is a story."

Zoe nodded eagerly. "Exactly."

Her voice dropped. "Do you think they'll ever figure out who did it?"

Emily's stomach tightened.

"They said they can't," Emily replied.

Zoe shrugged. "Yeah, but they always say that."

Emily stared at her desk.

Zoe kept talking anyway.

"My aunt thinks it was some older guy," she said. "Like, someone who saw her and—"

"Zoe," Emily said sharply.

Zoe blinked. "What?"

Emily forced her voice to soften. "Stop."

Zoe's mouth closed. For once, she looked uncertain.

"Sorry," she muttered.

Emily didn't answer.

At lunch, Blake found Emily by the edge of the courtyard where the wind cut between buildings.

He didn't say hi right away.

He just stepped into her space, close enough that the warmth of him registered through her coat.

"You look wrecked," he said quietly.

Emily gave a small shrug.

Blake's gaze moved over her face like he was reading something he wasn't going to name.

He didn't ask why.

He stepped in and pulled her close, his chin resting briefly against the top of her head before he let go.

Not gripping. Not demanding.

Present.

"You going this weekend?" he asked.

Emily nodded.

Blake's thumb moved once against the fabric, absent, steadying.

"I'll be there," he said. "If you want—"

"I don't know what I want," Emily said.

The words came out rough.

Blake didn't flinch.

"Okay," he said simply.

Then, after a beat: "You don't have to talk to me. But you don't have to stand by yourself either."

Emily swallowed.

She nodded once, because it was easier than speaking.

After school, she drove to her grandparents' house without deciding to.

The road out there felt longer than it had yesterday.

The sky had cleared, but the air held cold, sharp and clean.

Grandma's car sat in the driveway. Grandpa's truck, too.

Emily sat in her pickup for a moment, hands on the steering wheel, and watched the house.

She told herself she was only there to check on them.

She told herself she could leave if the door opened too quickly.

She got out anyway.

Grandpa answered the door.

"Hey, kiddo," he said, the same words as yesterday, as if repetition could keep life in order.

Emily forced a smile.

"Just stopping by," she said.

Grandpa nodded and stepped back. "Come in."

The house smelled like coffee and something sweet—brownies cooling somewhere.

Grandma was at the counter, her back to Emily. When she turned, her face was composed.

Not blank.

Controlled.

Her eyes met Emily's and held for one beat too long.

Emily felt her throat tighten.

Grandpa didn't notice. Or he pretended not to.

"You all set for this weekend?" he asked, moving to the table.

Grandma nodded once. "Mostly."

"Your grandma made brownies," Grandpa said to Emily, smiling faintly. "Like she always does when the town needs feeding."

Emily's chest tightened.

Because she could see it now: how ordinary offerings could be used to cover extraordinary things.

Grandma set a plate on the table without speaking.

Emily sat.

Grandpa talked about the county's plan to start filling next week, the way he always talked about practical things—like they could be managed with enough attention.

"They'll bring the level up slow," he said. "Controlled. Not like last time."

Emily's hands curled in her lap.

Grandma's hand paused on the edge of the counter.

"The last time was controlled too," she said quietly.

Grandpa looked up, surprised.

Grandma added, softer, "Just not the way people like to remember."

Grandpa nodded slowly. "Yeah," he said. "I suppose that's true."

Emily stared at the table.

She could feel Grandma watching her, not asking for anything, only acknowledging what they both carried now.

Grandpa stood and moved toward the living room.

"I'm gonna check the weather again," he said. "See if it'll hold for this weekend."

"Okay," Grandma said.

When he was out of the room, silence dropped like a curtain.

Emily's breath shook.

Grandma sat across from her.

They didn't speak.

They didn't need to.

Both of them knew what words did now.

After a while, Grandma said, very softly, "You're doing it."

Emily blinked.

"Doing what?"

Grandma's gaze held.

"Carrying it," she said.

Emily swallowed. "I don't know how."

Grandma nodded once, like that was the only honest answer.

"You don't learn it," she said. "You just...keep living."

Emily's eyes burned.

"I hate this," Emily whispered.

Grandma's mouth tightened.

"So do I," she said.

A beat.

"And I don't get to hate it more than you do."

Emily flinched, because it was true.

Grandma reached across the table and covered Emily's hand with hers.

Warm. Steady.

Not forgiving. Not asking.

Just present.

Footsteps sounded from the living room.

Grandma withdrew her hand at once, smooth and practiced.

Grandpa appeared in the doorway, holding his phone.

"Looks like it'll stay dry," he said. "Cold, though."

Grandma nodded. "People can wear coats."

Grandpa smiled faintly, as if that solved something.

Emily stood.

"I should go," she said.

Grandma rose too.

Grandpa followed them down the hall, still talking about parking at the overlook, the traffic, who might show.

Emily answered when she had to. Nodded when it was expected.

At the door, Grandpa touched her shoulder lightly.

"You drive safe," he said.

"I will," Emily replied.

Grandma stepped beside her.

They walked out together.

On the porch, Grandma kept her hand on Emily's arm a moment longer than necessary.

"This weekend," Grandma said quietly, "you can leave whenever you need to."

Emily nodded.

"And Emily," Grandma added, voice rough but steady, "don't let anyone make it into something it isn't."

Emily looked at her.

"What is it, then?" she whispered.

Grandma swallowed.

"A remembering," she said. "Not a fixing."

Emily nodded.

She got into her pickup and drove home.

The valley lay somewhere behind the trees, still open to the air, still exposed.

For a few more days.

Emily watched the road and held the truth in her chest.

Not as an accusation.

As a weight.

As practice.

As something she would have to carry through a crowd this weekend and not let anyone see.

She didn't know yet if she could.

But she was going to try.

CHAPTER FORTY ONE

Memorial

Saturday came with a kind of quiet the town didn't usually manage. Emily woke before her alarm and lay still, listening to the house settle. Somewhere down the hall, Kate shifted in her sleep, the faint creak of the mattress carrying through the hallway. In the kitchen, her mother moved with deliberate care, drawers opened and closed more gently than usual.

No one said much at breakfast.

The memorial flyer sat on the counter, weighted at one corner by a salt shaker, as if it might try to lift itself and leave.

Emily didn't mention the night at Grandma and Grandpa's. She didn't mention anything that would make her mother look at her too closely. She ate what she could and drank coffee she barely tasted.

Kate showed up with her sketchbook tucked under her arm, hair pulled back, eyes alert in a way that didn't look like nerves exactly—more like focus.

"You ready?" Kate asked.

Emily nodded.

Outside, the sky was low and pale, the kind of gray that made everything look rinsed. The air smelled like wet earth and cold metal. Rain had come and gone overnight, leaving the road dark and slick in patches.

They drove out of town with the radio off.

As they climbed toward the overlook, cars appeared more frequently—neighbors, people Emily recognized from school, older couples driving carefully, headlights on even though it was morning.

The overlook lot was already half full when Emily pulled in.

People stood in loose clusters near the railing, hands in pockets, shoulders hunched against the cold. A few kids from school hovered together, not talking much. Adults nodded to one another without enthusiasm, as if acknowledgment were the only appropriate offering.

Below, Evansville lay exposed.

The foundation lines looked sharper in the morning light, the pale shapes of streets and basements cutting through the darker earth. It didn't look like ruins, exactly. It looked like evidence.

A portable microphone stand had been set up near the edge, along with a small folding table holding a stack of programs. Someone had taped down the corners so the wind couldn't flip them over.

Kate reached for one, glanced at it, and folded it without comment.

Emily didn't take one.

She stood with Kate near the railing, close enough to see the bones of the town and far enough back that she didn't feel like she might fall into it.

People kept arriving.

Emily saw Zoe with her parents, Zoe's hair tucked into her coat collar. Zoe waved faintly, then moved closer, joining them without speaking.

Blake arrived a few minutes later, alone.

He didn't stay where he was.

He stepped closer to Emily, close enough that their sleeves brushed, then stayed there. After a moment, his hand found her wrist—not gripping, just resting there, warm and steady, like a question he wasn't asking out loud.

Emily didn't pull away.

"My grandpa didn't come," Blake said quietly. "He said he already did this once."

Emily nodded.

Blake's thumb moved once against the inside of her wrist, small and unconscious. "That makes sense."

She didn't ask what he meant by *did this*. It felt like a sentence with too many meanings.

A county official—someone Emily recognized from the library announcements and the careful radio voice—stepped to the microphone. The wind tugged at his jacket.

He cleared his throat.

"Thank you for coming," he began.

Emily listened without moving.

He spoke in measured phrases. About the discovery. About Clara Jennings' name. About how the investigation had reached its limit after so many decades. About the decision to begin refilling the reservoir the following week.

"Before that happens," he said, "we wanted to give the community a chance to remember. To acknowledge what was lost."

Emily's hands went cold.

He said Clara's name once, clearly, and then moved on.

A pastor spoke next—someone older, voice soft, careful not to turn the moment into a sermon. He spoke about grief that waited. About families who carried questions longer than anyone should have to.

Emily watched faces as they listened.

Some people looked down. Some stared out at the exposed foundations. A few held hands. No one cried loudly. Most didn't cry at all. It was too old for that, too far away. And still—something in the air held.

Then the pastor invited anyone who wanted to come forward.

One by one, people did.

An elderly woman stepped up first, holding a small bouquet of wildflowers. She set them on the table and stood still for a moment, head bowed, then walked away.

A man in a worn cap placed a faded photograph beside the flowers. He lingered longer than he needed to, fingers resting on the edge of the photo as if it might slide away.

Others followed.

Tokens. Notes. A ribbon. A folded letter sealed with tape.

Emily stayed where she was, Blake still beside her. When she shifted her weight, his shoulder brushed hers again, deliberate this time.

Kate's pencil moved quietly across a page in her sketchbook. She drew with her head down, intent, as if the act of making lines could anchor the scene to something that wouldn't vanish.

Then Grandma and Grandpa arrived.

Emily felt it before she saw them—some subtle widening in the crowd. They walked carefully through the clusters of people, Grandpa's hand light at Grandma's elbow.

Grandma's face was composed. Not blank. Controlled in the way it always was when she needed to be.

They didn't come directly to Emily. They didn't look for her.

They waited near the table until the line thinned.

When it was their turn, Grandpa stepped forward first.

He held a single red rose.

The color looked impossible against the gray morning, bright and clean like it hadn't come from the same world as the exposed valley below.

He set it gently on the table.

He didn't bow his head. He didn't close his eyes. He just stood there for a long moment, hand resting near the flower as if he didn't want to let it go.

Then he stepped back.

Grandma moved forward.

She held a single yellow rose.

She placed it beside the red one with care, aligning the stems as if order could mean something.

For a moment, her composure slipped. Not visibly to anyone else. Just in the way her shoulders tightened and then released.

She brushed her fingers lightly over the petals, then pulled her hand away.

Then she stepped back to Grandpa's side.

Emily's throat tightened.

Blake's hand tightened slightly around her wrist. Not possessive. Just present.

She turned her face slightly so no one would see.

Beside her, Kate paused her drawing and looked up, eyes tracking the roses.

"Why two?" Kate whispered.

Emily swallowed.

"Two kinds of remembering," she said quietly.

Kate nodded once and went back to her sketchbook.

The crowd began to loosen after that, people drifting back toward their cars, voices low.

Zoe touched Emily's sleeve.

"You okay?" she asked.

Emily nodded. "Yeah."

It was the easiest lie she'd ever told.

Blake stayed at the railing, still close.

"They're going to cover it again," he said.

Emily nodded.

"Does it feel wrong?" he asked.

Emily didn't answer. She didn't know which part he meant.

Behind them, Grandpa spoke to someone Emily didn't recognize, his voice polite, ordinary. Grandma stood beside him, hands folded, listening.

No one looked at them the way Emily did.

No one saw what the yellow rose meant. No one saw the truth standing quietly beside the red.

Kate had drifted back to find their parents, sketchbook tucked under her arm, leaving Emily at the railing.

When the wind sharpened and the crowd thinned, voices softened further, as if the town instinctively knew this wasn't something to leave loudly.

Emily stayed where she was.

She looked once more at the table near the railing.

The roses lay side by side.

Red for first love.

Yellow for friendship.

And between them, something else—unspoken, unnamed, held.

She understood then that the space mattered as much as the flowers themselves. What hadn't been said. What couldn't be corrected. What would never be explained out loud.

Blake remained close, not touching her, not asking if she was ready. Just present in the way that didn't demand anything.

Below them, the exposed valley lay quiet, its lines sharp in the thin light, waiting to be covered again.

Emily held the truth in her chest.

Not as an accusation.

As a decision.

CHAPTER FORTY TWO

Custody

They stayed after most people left.

Not because there was anything more to see, but because leaving felt like a choice that mattered.

The overlook thinned in stages. Cars pulled out slowly, tires crunching over gravel. Voices stayed low. People nodded without stopping, as if conversation might disturb something that had finally been set down.

Emily stood near the railing, hands buried in her coat pockets. The valley lay open below them, its lines sharp in the thinning light.

Blake stood beside her. Close, but not touching.

When the lot was nearly empty, he glanced toward the road where the last of the cars had turned back toward town.

"You okay to head out?" he asked.

Emily nodded. "Yeah." Then she kicked a stone with her right foot. "No."

The wind sharpened, colder now without bodies to break it.

Blake shifted his weight. Then he held his hand out.

Not rushed. Not expectant.

Just there.

Emily looked at it for a moment, then slid her fingers into his.

He didn't squeeze. He didn't pull.

They walked together toward his truck, their steps matched without effort.

At the passenger side, Blake let go long enough to open the door for her. Emily hesitated—just a beat—then climbed in.

"Thanks," she said quietly.

He nodded and closed the door before circling around.

As they pulled out of the lot, Emily looked back once.

The overlook stood nearly empty now. The folding table still stood near the railing, unattended. The railing was bare.

The valley waited.

* * *

The heater hummed softly as Blake drove.

Emily folded her hands in her lap. Her breathing lagged slightly behind where it should have been, shallow and uneven, like her body hadn't quite caught up with where she was.

They drove in silence for a mile.

Then Emily spoke.

"It was my grandma," she said. Her voice stayed low, even. "Martha."

Blake's hands tightened slightly on the wheel, but he didn't interrupt.

"She and Clara both loved my grandpa," Emily went on. "Not the same way. Not with the same expectations. But he mattered to both of them."

She swallowed.

"My grandpa and Clara argued that night," Emily said. "After graduation. She wanted him to leave with her. He told her he couldn't."

Blake glanced at her, then back to the road.

"She was angry," Emily said. "She was crying. And she went into the water while she was still yelling at him."

Her hands curled in her lap.

"My grandma followed her," Emily continued. "She was upset, too. Hurt. Afraid of what Clara was saying—of what it would do to him."

She paused.

"They scuffled in the water," Emily said. "Not shouting. Grabbing. Pushing. Clara turned on her."

Blake's jaw tightened, but he said nothing.

"Grandma hit her," Emily said. "And when she understood what she'd done—when there was no fixing it—she made a choice."

The words felt heavier once spoken, but steadier too.

"She swam her down," Emily said. "She put her in the cellar."

A shiver rose along Emily's spine as she heard her grandma's words in her head, "I tried to move her hair out of her face, but it kept floating up around her head, as out of control as I felt in that moment."

Silence settled between them, not empty but full—like something that had finally been placed where it belonged.

After a moment, Blake said quietly, "That's...a lot to live with."

Emily nodded. "She didn't mean to keep her from leaving. She meant to stop her from hurting him."

"And instead," Blake said.

"And instead," Emily finished, "she lived with it."

***

They turned onto a narrower road, trees closing in on both sides.

After a minute, Blake said, "We're not going straight back."

Emily blinked. "Where are we going?"

"To my grandpa's," he said. "Just for a minute."

Emily didn't argue.

***

Earl's porch light cast a dull yellow square across the gravel.

Blake shut off the engine and glanced at Emily.

"This isn't about new information," he said. "I know you've seen the boxes."

Emily nodded.

"I just think it might help to see them now," he added. "After today."

She understood.

They went in together.

The house smelled like coffee and paper. The boxes sat where they always had, stacked neatly against the wall. No labels. No dates. Just weight.

Emily stood still.

Earl noticed.

"People think I kept those because I didn't know what to do with them," he said. "That's not it."

He rested his hand on the top box.

"I knew exactly what they were," he said. "And who they belonged to."

Emily swallowed.

"I couldn't deliver them," Earl continued. "But I couldn't throw them away either. That would've meant deciding they were done mattering."

He looked at Emily then.

"That's not hiding," he said. "That's custody."

Something shifted in Emily—not relief, but recognition.

Blake watched her quietly.

"This is what I meant," he said softly. "Holding isn't always erasing."

Emily nodded. "Sometimes it's the opposite."

They didn't stay long.

* * *

Back at the overlook, Emily's pickup sat alone near the edge of the lot.

Blake parked beside it and waited as she unlocked the door.

She climbed in and turned the key.

The engine coughed once, then caught.

She stayed there a moment, hands on the wheel, breathing until her chest steadied.

Blake didn't move.

When she looked up, he was still there, watching to make sure she was okay.

Emily got out and crossed the few steps between them.

She reached for his hand again—brief, deliberate.

"Thank you," she said.

He squeezed once. "Anytime."

He stayed until she pulled away.

Emily drove with both hands on the wheel.

The valley lay hidden behind trees now, already slipping back toward silence.

The truth stayed with her.

Not as a secret.

Not as an accusation.

As something entrusted.

CHAPTER FORTY THREE

Still Water

The first markers appeared along the road two days later.

Emily noticed them on her drive to school—thin orange flags pressed into the shoulder at regular intervals, each one numbered in black marker. They weren't warnings. They weren't barriers.

They were measurements.

At a stop sign, she rolled her window down and watched one of the flags tremble in the breeze. It looked temporary. Almost flimsy. But it stayed where it was.

At school, no one talked about the memorial anymore.

That part, apparently, was finished.

Zoe complained about a chemistry quiz. Someone else argued about a locker mix-up. A teacher lost track of the attendance sheet and started over without apology.

The town slipped back into its habits with impressive efficiency.

In history class, Mr. Tolland erased half the board and left the other half untouched.

"We'll finish this unit next week," he said. "No sense rushing."

Emily stared at the chalked word *relocated* until it blurred.

Rushing, she thought, had never really been the problem.

After school, she didn't go straight home.

She drove the long way, looping past the marina road. The gates were still up from when the lake had been drained—temporary fencing, a sign zip-tied to it, curling at the edges from wind and sun.

CLOSED UNTIL FURTHER NOTICE

Beyond it, the docks sat crooked and dry, their pilings exposed like bones. Everything looked paused rather than abandoned, waiting for water to return and pretend it had never left.

Emily didn't stop. She didn't need to.

At dinner, her father talked about runoff and timing, about how controlled refills were safer than the old way.

"They'll bring it up slow," he said. "Measure as they go."

Her mother nodded. "That's the whole point."

Kate pushed peas around her plate. "Do you think it remembers?"

Everyone looked at her.

"The town," Kate said. "Do you think it remembers being a town?"

Her parents exchanged a look meant to soften the moment.

"I don't think places remember," her father said gently.

Emily kept eating.

Later, in her room, she opened her notebook and didn't write anything in it. She let it rest on the bed, pages blank, waiting for something that wouldn't arrive cleanly.

What she knew now didn't fit into sentences.

It existed as weight. As sequence. As consequence.

She thought of Grandma aligning the yellow rose beside the red. Of Earl's hand resting on the boxes like a promise. Of Blake's word—*custody*—settling somewhere deep and immovable.

People would say the refill erased things.

Emily understood now that wasn't true.

It only changed who was responsible for remembering.

Her phone buzzed.

Blake: You okay?

She stared at the screen longer than necessary.

Emily: I think I'm figuring out what I'm holding.

A pause.

Blake: Yeah. That sounds about right.

Emily set the phone face-down on the bed and lay back, staring at the ceiling.

A soft knock came at her door.

Not loud. Not tentative either. Just Kate.

"Em?"

Emily didn't answer right away, but she didn't tell her to go away.

The door opened a few inches.

Kate stood there with her sketchbook tucked against her hip, pajama pants already on, hair pulled loose like she'd decided sleep could wait.

"You've been weird all week," Kate said. Not accusing. Observational. "Like...quiet weird. Not normal weird."

Emily huffed a breath despite herself.

Kate took that as permission and came in, sitting on the edge of the bed without asking.

They stayed like that for a moment. The room held them easily—the way shared spaces do when they've been shared a long time.

"You don't have to tell me," Kate said finally. "I just need to know if this is the kind of thing where I should stop joking around you."

Emily closed her eyes.

"That bad?" Kate asked.

Emily opened them again. Looked at her sister. At the familiar seriousness she saved for things that mattered.

"It's not about me," Emily said carefully.

Kate nodded. "It never is when you do this."

Emily smiled faintly.

Kate bumped her shoulder with her own. "I don't like it when you carry stuff alone," she said. "You get all...tight."

Emily swallowed.

"I'm okay," she said. "I promise."

Kate studied her for a long moment, then leaned back on her hands.

"Okay," she said. "But if you stop sleeping, or you start snapping at people, or you look like you're about to disappear into your own head—"

"I won't," Emily said.

Kate raised an eyebrow.

"—much," Emily amended.

That earned her a small smile.

Kate stood. "I'll take that."

She paused at the door, hand on the frame.

"Whatever it is," she said, quieter now, "I know you're not making it worse. You never do."

Then she left, the door closing softly behind her.

Emily stayed where she was, the room feeling different now—not lighter, exactly, but less sealed.

Not everything had to be spoken to be shared.

Outside, the night stayed quiet. No urgency. No spectacle.

Just time doing what it always did.

Moving forward.

Whether anyone was ready or not.

CHAPTER FORTY FOUR

Watching the Line

Emily waited for Kate outside the school, leaning against the side of her pickup while buses pulled away one by one. Students drifted past in loose clusters, talking about homework, rides, weekend plans—ordinary things that moved easily through the afternoon.

Kate emerged last, sketchbook tucked under her arm like it always was when she didn't want to think too hard about what she was doing next.

She spotted Emily and lifted her chin slightly in acknowledgment, then crossed the lot.

"You're going up there again," Kate said as she reached her.

It wasn't a question.

Emily nodded. "Yeah."

Kate adjusted the strap of her backpack. "Okay."

No *why*. No pause. Just agreement, which somehow carried more weight than curiosity.

They climbed into the truck and pulled out of the lot without turning the radio on.

The road out of town curved gently, familiar enough that Emily barely had to think about it. The land opened as they climbed, trees thinning, the sky stretching wider above them.

Emily parked where she had before.

They got out together.

The reservoir looked different already. Not dramatically—just enough that Emily felt it before she could name it. The exposed ground was darker, slicker in places where it had been dry days earlier. The waterline sat higher along the far edge, subtle but undeniable.

Kate stepped up onto the low concrete barrier and stood still.

"It's moving," she said.

Emily nodded. "Yeah."

Kate squinted, shading her eyes with one hand. "I thought they weren't opening the valves until Monday."

"They aren't," Emily said. "This is just runoff and seep—what happens when everything's getting ready."

Kate absorbed that.

She opened her sketchbook but didn't start drawing right away. Instead, she studied the line where water met earth, how it curved differently than before.

"Wasn't there more yesterday?" Kate asked.

Emily swallowed. "There was."

Kate didn't comment. She just turned to a clean page and began to sketch, pencil moving in short, careful strokes. She didn't draw the whole valley. Just one section. Just the edge.

Emily stood beside her, hands in her jacket pockets, watching the place where the cellar had been.

There was nothing to see now.

Only water. Only surface.

Kate glanced up. "You always stand right there."

Emily hadn't realized she did.

"Yeah," she said quietly.

Kate went back to her drawing.

After a while, she said, "Mom thinks this makes things better."

Emily exhaled slowly. "Does she?"

"She said people need closure." Kate paused. "I don't think this is that."

Emily looked at her.

Kate shrugged. "It just looks like covering."

That landed harder than Emily expected.

They stayed until the wind cut through their jackets and Kate's fingers stiffened around the pencil.

On the drive home, Kate didn't show Emily the drawing.

That night, Kate knocked once on Emily's door before coming in.

Emily was sitting on the edge of her bed, shoes still on, backpack untouched on the floor.

Kate sat beside her without asking.

"You don't have to tell me," Kate said. "But you are holding something."

Emily closed her eyes.

Kate continued, softer now. "I can tell because you're being careful in a way you aren't usually careful."

Emily laughed once, breathless. "That's... accurate."

Kate leaned back on her hands. "I'm not asking to know it. I just don't want you thinking you have to carry it by yourself."

Emily opened her eyes.

The truth pressed against her ribs—not ready to come out, but no longer sharp in the same way.

"Thanks," she said.

Kate nodded, satisfied. She stood and paused at the door.

"You should let me draw it sometime," she added. "Whatever it is."

Emily watched her leave.

Later, lying in bed, Emily thought about the waterline.

How it moved without rushing.

How it didn't ask permission.

How it made its way back by inches, not waves.

The reservoir wasn't erasing anything yet.

It was reminding the ground what it had agreed to hold.

Emily turned onto her side and let herself believe—just for tonight—that holding something didn't always mean hiding it.

Sometimes it meant standing beside someone else and watching the line together.

CHAPTER FORTY FIVE

Spring Work

By early spring, the reservoir had learned how to look like itself again. Not the version people waited for in July, when boats crowded the marina and the shoreline filled with noise—but the outline. The shape that let the town pretend nothing unusual had ever happened beneath the surface.

Spring arrived at school without ceremony.

The air in the hallways shifted first—less bite, more dampness. Boots thudded less heavily. Coats disappeared into lockers instead of staying zipped to chests. Someone propped open a door at lunch and let cold air roll through the building like permission.

Emily shut her locker and felt the click of the latch settle something in her chest.

A small sound. Final.

Down the hall, a freshman sprinted past in socks, backpack bouncing, clearly late and clearly unconcerned. A teacher called after him without much conviction.

Normal had returned.

Emily leaned back against the lockers for a second longer than necessary, then pushed off.

"Do you ever think," Zoe said beside her, voice dry as dust, "that this town would collapse under the weight of its own secrets if everyone stopped pretending not to notice things?"

Emily huffed quietly. "No. I think it would just get quieter."

Zoe glanced at her. "That's worse."

Emily smiled despite herself.

Zoe stood with her binder tucked against her side, eyes sharp, posture relaxed in the way that meant she'd already clocked every exit. She didn't pry. She didn't soften her voice. She wasn't tall, but she carried herself like she took up exactly the space she meant to—dark hair pulled back cleanly, small earrings catching light when she turned her head. Even in boots and denim, there was something deliberate about her, nothing accidental. When she shifted her weight, it was balanced and ready.

She just *noticed*.

"You're going up there," Zoe said, not asking.

Emily hesitated, then nodded. "Yeah."

Zoe exhaled through her nose. "Figures."

That was it. No commentary. No warning. Just acknowledgment.

They moved with the current of students toward the doors.

Blake was waiting near the exit, backpack slung over one shoulder, jacket half-zipped like he hadn't bothered to finish getting ready. When he saw Emily, his posture shifted—subtle, instinctive.

He didn't wave.

He waited.

Emily stepped into his space without thinking, and his arm slid easily around her shoulders, familiar as breath. She leaned into him just enough to register the contact.

"Hey," he said.

"Hey."

Zoe stopped in front of them and arched an eyebrow. "I see we're doing the extremely public version of not talking."

Blake smiled faintly. Emily rolled her eyes.

"You coming?" Blake asked Zoe.

Zoe made a face. "I'm not emotionally prepared to supervise you two near a body of water."

"Fair," Emily said.

They stepped outside together into the sharp spring air.

* * *

Emily waited by her truck while Kate crossed the lot, sketchbook tucked under her arm, jacket unzipped despite the cold. Kate climbed in without a word, tossing her backpack at her feet.

"You're going," Kate said.

Emily started the engine. "Yeah."

"Okay."

No why. No argument. Just acceptance.

Blake pulled out behind them. Zoe followed a beat later.

No coordination needed. No signals. Just habit.

* * *

The overlook lot was mostly empty.

Not deserted—nothing ever was—but quiet enough that the wind made itself known.

Emily parked and shut off the engine. For a second she stayed with her hands on the wheel, feeling the soft tick of cooling metal and the way her own breath still tried to measure things.

Kate was already unbuckling.

Zoe was already scanning the lot like she was checking for witnesses.

Blake just waited—patient in a way that didn't ask questions.

They stepped out together.

The reservoir sat higher now. Not full. Not finished. But close enough that the place had started to look familiar again, like it was putting its face back on for the town.

Kate climbed onto the low concrete barrier and opened her sketchbook. The wind caught at her braid, pulling loose strands across her face and setting the auburn briefly alight in the sun. She looked small up there—angular, unfinished—like a year still in progress. When she lifted her chin toward the waterline, her eyes held the same unsettled green, storm-washed and searching.

She didn't speak right away. She just studied the edge where water met earth, then put pencil to paper with the quiet determination she had when something mattered.

Zoe stood a few feet back, hands in her pockets, gaze moving along the shoreline in slow, deliberate sweeps.

"This is wildly scenic," she said. "I understand why people come here to pretend they're emotionally stable."

Kate snorted without looking up.

Emily stepped out of the truck and pulled her braid forward over one shoulder, fingers separating the strands and weaving them tighter. It was something she did when she needed her thoughts to fall into order. She stood taller than both Kate and Zoe, her height long settled into her now, easy and unself-conscious. There was strength in the way she held herself—legs steady, shoulders loose but certain.

Blake stayed beside Emily. Not hovering. Not guarding. Just there—arm around her shoulders in that easy, familiar way that meant he wasn't afraid of the weight anymore.

For a second, she held herself the way she always did. Then she let herself lean into him.

Emily let herself lean into him.

The wind moved across the surface and the water answered in small, constant sounds—nothing dramatic. Nothing cinematic. Just the lake doing what lakes did: holding and moving at the same time.

Emily's eyes found the spot again.

Not because there was anything to see, but because her body remembered where to look.

Zoe glanced at her, then back at the water.

"Okay," she said, quieter now. "I get it."

Emily didn't ask what she meant. Zoe rarely explained herself when she didn't have to.

Kate paused long enough to flex her fingers, then kept drawing. "The line looks different," she said, mostly to herself.

"It does," Emily agreed.

Blake's hand shifted at Emily's upper arm—one small squeeze. Anchor, not question.

They stayed until the cold started to push through their clothes and the wind made Kate's pages flutter.

On the way back to the vehicles, Zoe slowed beside Emily.

"If either of you decide to have a profound moment," she said, "please remember I'm allergic to sincerity in direct sunlight."

Emily's mouth tilted. "We'll put it in the shade."

Zoe nodded, satisfied, and peeled off toward her car.

Kate climbed back into Emily's truck, sketchbook closed against her chest like she was keeping something safe.

Blake walked Emily to her door.

He didn't hesitate.

He leaned in and kissed her—brief, easy, his mouth brushing lightly over hers like it had done this a hundred times before. No urgency. No spectacle.

"You okay?" he asked softly when he pulled back.

Emily nodded. "Yeah."

"Text me when you get home."

"I will."

He squeezed her hand once before stepping back.

Emily watched him go, then climbed in and drove Kate home.

CHAPTER FORTY SIX

What Holds

By May, Emily stopped checking the waterline on purpose.

Not because it didn't matter anymore—but because she no longer needed to prove to herself that it was still there. The refill had become a fact instead of a question. Something measured by engineers and reported in inches on the radio, not something that lived in her chest.

School narrowed.

Teachers mentioned finals. Lockers filled with half-forgotten jackets and notes folded too many times. The hallway outside the office smelled like copy paper and stress.

Emily leaned against her locker and flipped through her phone, not really reading anything.

Zoe appeared beside her like she always did—unannounced, precise.

"You've entered the phase where everyone pretends productivity will save them," Zoe said. "It won't."

Emily smiled faintly. "You're very comforting."

"I know."

Blake came up on Emily's other side, close enough that his shoulder pressed into hers automatically. He didn't say anything at first. Just rested his weight there, familiar and solid.

Emily let herself lean back.

Zoe watched them with mild amusement. "I see the emotional-support-boyfriend program is still operational."

Blake grinned. "Fully funded."

"Shocking," Zoe said. "Given the town's budget priorities."

They walked together toward class, the three of them falling into step without discussion. It wasn't intentional anymore. It was habit.

That was the part Emily kept noticing — how habits formed quietly around weight.

***

After school, they sat on the low wall by the parking lot instead of leaving right away.

Someone practiced trumpet badly inside the band room. A group of freshmen argued about rides. The world went on without ceremony.

Emily's phone buzzed.

Unknown Number: You still watching?

Her thumb hovered.

Zoe clocked it instantly. "That the ghost, or the universe?"

Emily exhaled. "The first one."

Blake didn't crowd her. He just stayed where he was, arm resting along the back of the wall behind her shoulders.

Emily: I know where to look now.

A pause.

Unknown Number: Good.

Nothing else.

Emily locked the screen and slid the phone back into her pocket.

Zoe tilted her head. "That's it?"

"That's it."

Zoe considered. "Efficient. I respect that."

Blake shifted his weight. "I've got weights," he said, already standing. "I'll text you when I get done."

Emily nodded. "Okay."

He didn't linger. Just gave her shoulder a light squeeze and headed toward the side doors.

They were sitting on the low concrete wall behind the school, the one everyone pretended wasn't for loitering. The afternoon was clear and cold in that way spring liked best—sunny, bright, sharp around the edges.

Zoe had her binder open on her lap, not reading it. Emily noticed that first.

"You're hovering," Zoe said, without looking up.

Emily frowned. "I'm sitting."

Zoe flipped a page she didn't need. "You're sitting like someone waiting for a verdict."

Emily exhaled. "I hate when you do that."

"Then stop being predictable," Zoe said mildly.

They sat in silence for a moment. Wind rattled the flagpole. Somewhere inside the building, a bell rang too early and stopped.

Zoe closed her binder.

"This isn't about finals," she said. "Or Blake. Or the lake itself."

Emily's jaw tightened.

Zoe leaned back on her hands, eyes on the sky. "You stopped asking questions out loud," she continued. "That's usually when people stop believing the answers they're getting."

Emily stared at the cracked pavement in front of her. A weed pushed up through one of the seams, stubborn and green.

"It wasn't an accident," she said.

The words landed between them. Solid. Unadorned.

Zoe didn't gasp. Didn't shift. Didn't even look at her right away.

After a beat, she nodded once.

"Okay," she said.

Emily turned to her. "That's it?"

Zoe glanced over then, expression sharp but steady. "You weren't offering details," she said. "You were offering a fact."

Emily swallowed. "Someone I love was involved."

Zoe's mouth tightened—not in judgment, but concentration. She nodded again, slower this time.

"And you're not asking me to do anything," Zoe said. "Which means you're already doing it yourself."

Emily let out a shaky breath she hadn't realized she'd been holding. "I don't know what to do with it," she admitted.

Zoe considered her for a long moment.

"I don't need names," she said finally. "And I don't need the whole story." She paused. "I just need to know whether this ends with you disappearing into it."

Emily shook her head. "No."

Zoe watched her closely, like she was verifying data.

"Good," she said. "Because that would be annoying."

Emily huffed a laugh, surprised by it.

Zoe stood and slung her binder under her arm. "You're standing on a fault line," she said. "That doesn't make you responsible for the earthquake."

Emily looked up at her. "You're not... mad?"

Zoe snorted softly. "I'm not simple."

She hesitated, then added, quieter, "And I'm not going anywhere."

That did it. Emily's eyes burned, fast and sharp.

Zoe grimaced. "Don't cry. I just made a choice, not a speech."

Emily laughed, wiping at her face. "Thank you."

Zoe shrugged. "We all carry things," she said. "Some of us just label the boxes better."

She started toward the parking lot, then glanced back.

"For the record," she added, "I still reserve the right to be sarcastic about this forever."

Emily smiled. "I'd be disappointed if you weren't."

Zoe nodded once, satisfied, and kept walking.

Emily stayed where she was for a moment longer, the truth still heavy—but no longer hers alone.

* * *

Kate was waiting at the truck when Emily finally headed out, sketchbook hugged to her chest like always.

"You're late," Kate said.

"Sorry."

Kate shrugged. "I drew instead of worrying."

Emily smiled. "Healthy."

Kate climbed in, tossed her bag down, then paused.

"You're not lighter," she said, staring out the windshield. "But you're steadier."

Emily blinked. "That's very specific."

Kate shrugged. "I notice things."

They drove home with the windows cracked, spring air cold but clean.

Inside the house, dinner happened. Homework happened. Normal happened.

Later, Blake came by and stayed longer than planned. Not because of anything dramatic — just because no one told him to leave.

He kissed Emily in the doorway before heading out, easy and familiar, like it belonged there.

It did.

That night, Emily lay in bed and thought about the difference between holding and being held.

She understood now that one didn't cancel out the other.

Outside, the town stayed quiet. The reservoir continued its work.

And Emily, finally, let herself believe that knowing the truth didn't mean standing alone with it.

Sometimes it just meant learning how to live while carrying it — and letting other people walk beside you while you did.

CHAPTER FORTY SEVEN

What Stays

By late spring, the reservoir had stopped drawing attention to itself. It was full enough now that people stopped talking about levels and measurements. The waterline blended back into the shoreline the way it always had, erasing the markers first, then the memory of them. From the road, it looked like it always did—quiet, reflective, unremarkable.

Emily noticed the change not because anyone announced it, but because no one did.

At school, things continued the way they were supposed to.

Teachers handed back papers. Coaches reminded seniors about eligibility forms. A sign went up near the office with the graduation schedule—same weekend, same time it had always been. Memorial Day. Sunday. Like it had been decided long before any of them were born.

Zoe leaned against Emily's locker one afternoon, arms crossed, eyes scanning the hallway like she was watching a system run.

"No true-crime vans," she said. "No podcast people lurking by the gas station. I'm calling it a win."

Emily shut her locker. "You're disappointed."

"Only academically," Zoe replied. "I like my mysteries with footnotes."

They walked together toward the doors, absorbed into the current of students heading out. No one stopped them. No one stared. A few people nodded hello. Someone asked Emily about a math assignment she'd missed last week.

Normal, she'd learned, didn't mean unaffected. It meant practiced.

At home, Kate spread her homework across the kitchen table, sketchbook tucked off to one side like it was waiting its turn.

"They're already talking about graduation weekend," Kate said, pencil moving steadily. "Like it's a done deal."

Emily poured water into a glass and leaned against the counter. "It usually is."

Kate frowned. "It feels early."

"It always does," Emily said. "Then suddenly it's not."

Kate considered that, then nodded, satisfied enough. She went back to her work without pressing further.

That night, Emily sat on her bed with her window cracked open, the air cool and damp with spring melt. She could hear the house settling, the familiar sounds of dishes being put away, her parents' voices low but easy.

Her phone buzzed.

Blake: You still alive in there?

Emily smiled.

Emily: Barely. Math homework is attempting to end me.

Blake: Tragic. Need backup?

Emily: Not tonight.

A pause.

Blake: Okay. Tomorrow, then.

She set the phone down.

Outside, the night moved the way it always had. No rush. No hesitation. Just forward.

Emily lay back and stared at the ceiling.

She thought about how little had actually changed, and how everything had.

The truth hadn't rearranged the world. It hadn't demanded anything from anyone but her. The town kept functioning. The lake kept filling. People kept living.

What stayed, she realized, wasn't the story itself.

It was who carried it.

In the next room, Kate turned a page.

Emily closed her eyes and let herself rest in the sound of it—the ordinary, ongoing proof that life didn't stop for understanding. It only made room for it.

Spring would keep moving.

Graduation would come when it always did.

And Emily would live with what she knew —not alone, and not in silence, but as part of the life that kept going anyway.

CHAPTER FORTY EIGHT

Commencement

Graduation morning arrived without spectacle.

The sky was overcast but high, the kind of gray that held instead of threatened. Emily stood in her bedroom doorway while her mother adjusted the folds of her gown, tugging once at the shoulder seam like she was checking the fit of something she'd been holding in her hands for years.

"Turn," her mother said.

Emily did.

Her mother nodded once, satisfied, and stepped back.

Kate leaned against the hallway wall, arms crossed, sketchbook tucked under one elbow. "You look like you're about to do something important," she said.

Emily huffed. "I am."

Kate tilted her head. "Weird."

Their mother appeared holding a single corsage, the flowers wrapped in damp paper like they'd been handled more than necessary.

"Okay," she said. "Come here."

She pinned it to Emily's gown with careful fingers. She did it the same way she always did when something mattered: quietly, like steadiness was a choice she was making on purpose.

"There," her mother said softly.

Kate watched. Didn't comment.

* * *

Behind her, footsteps sounded, and she knew it was Blake before she turned—because his voice had become the easiest thing in her world to recognize.

"You hiding," he said.

It wasn't a question. It was a fact delivered with a faint, crooked kind of warmth.

Emily turned.

Blake's cap sat slightly too high on his head, like he'd shoved it on without checking. The gown made him look older and younger at the same time—broad-shouldered, tall, still the same boy she'd known in the halls, now pressed into a version of himself that looked like the future.

He stepped into her space like it belonged to him now. Comfortable. Familiar. His hand brushed her elbow, then settled at her waist like he wasn't asking permission anymore.

Emily let herself lean into him for half a second.

Zoe watched them with mild disgust. "Truly inspiring," she said. "I'm going to throw up."

Blake grinned. "Love you too."

"You don't," Zoe said. "You tolerate me because I keep Emily from spiraling."

Emily made a face. "Am I spiraling."

Zoe's expression stayed bland. "Not today. Gold star."

Blake's hand tightened once, gentle. "You good?" he asked Emily quietly.

Emily nodded. And meant it.

Not because it was easy. Because she'd learned the difference between drowning and standing in water that didn't move.

A teacher herded them toward the double doors that led to the hallway. Names were being lined up. Orders were being checked. Someone's tassel got untangled. Someone else whispered that they were going to faint, like they'd rehearsed the drama.

Emily heard her name—her last name—spoken by someone with a clipboard, and it felt surreal in the simplest way.

Like: *This is still happening. Life is still doing what it does.*

They lined up.

The hallway outside the gym was cooler. Lockers were shut, silent. Someone had taped up photos of the seniors—baby pictures and awkward middle school snapshots—along the wall. Emily caught sight of hers in a quick glance: missing front teeth, sunburnt nose, squinting into the camera like she couldn't trust it.

Zoe snorted beside her. "You look like you were born skeptical."

"I was," Emily murmured.

Blake leaned in behind her. "You were born judging," he said into her hair, low enough only she could hear.

Emily huffed a laugh that loosened something in her ribs.

Then the principal stepped to the mic, and the gym noise shifted into the ceremonial hush people reserved for moments they wanted to believe mattered more than the rest.

They walked in.

The applause hit like weather—loud, unavoidable, a swell that filled the room and made Emily's face go hot. People stood. Phones rose. Voices called names that weren't allowed to be called out, anyway.

Emily kept her eyes forward.

But she felt the bleachers. Felt the weight of the town watching, proud in the uncomplicated way it could still be proud of something.

She wondered—briefly, sharply—if this was what Grandpa remembered from his graduation night.

The gym full. The noise. The sense that something was beginning.

And then, later, the doors.

The argument outside.

The place where watching ended.

Emily's stomach tightened.

Blake's hand brushed her wrist as they sat, just a small reminder that she was not alone in this row, in this year, in this moment.

Speeches happened.

The valedictorian said something earnest about roots and wings. The principal said something about potential. The superintendent mispronounced one name and apologized, laughing, like that fixed it.

Emily listened without really listening.

She watched people instead.

She watched Zoe's mouth twitch every time someone tried to get poetic.

She watched Blake's jaw tighten when the athletic director spoke—because Blake didn't like being talked about like he was a story people had made up for themselves.

She watched her grandma in the bleachers, hands folded, posture perfect, eyes on the floor for long stretches—then lifting, once in a while, like she was forcing herself to stay in the room.

When they started calling names, time turned strange.

People stood. Walked. Shook hands. Took diplomas. Smiled too hard. Sat back down.

Emily's name came sooner than she expected.

She stood, gown swaying around her legs, the cap's elastic pulling slightly against her hair. She walked across the court like she was moving through a memory.

Applause rose. Her mother's voice cut through it—sharp, proud. Kate whistled, because Kate couldn't do anything normally.

Emily shook the principal's hand. Took the diploma. Turned.

For one second, her eyes landed on the gym doors again.

Just doors.

Just air.

But the past was layered here like paint.

She walked back to her seat and sat down, heart beating too fast.

Zoe went next.

When Zoe's name was called, the applause that rose wasn't the loudest. It was the most specific—teachers clapping like they knew exactly what they were sending out of the building, parents smiling like they were relieved she'd survived their town.

Zoe walked with her shoulders back, expression calm, like she was collecting evidence.

When she sat back down, she leaned toward Emily and murmured, "If anyone asks me to 'come back and visit,' I'm going to fake my own death."

Emily's laugh came out a little too loud. Zoe looked pleased.

Blake's name—when it came—shifted the room.

It shouldn't have. It was still just a diploma. Still just a walk across a gym floor.

But the town loved a scholarship like it loved a good harvest. Proof. Outcome. Something it could point at and say, *See. We made something*.

The announcer said it clearly, because people liked to hear it: Montana State. Football. Scholarship.

The bleachers erupted.

Blake didn't smile big. He didn't wave. He walked like he was in control of himself, took the diploma, nodded once, and came back to his seat like none of it could claim him.

When he sat, his knee bumped Emily's. His hand slid under the edge of her gown and found her fingers.

He squeezed once.

Not celebration.

Anchor.

After the last name, caps were tossed.

The moment was chaotic in the way people tried to pretend was spontaneous.

Emily didn't throw hers. She held it.

Zoe did not throw hers either. She watched other people do it like she was studying a minor cultural ritual and deciding whether it deserved to exist.

Blake tossed his, caught it badly, and laughed when it hit him in the shoulder.

Emily looked at him and felt something lift—just slightly—inside her chest.

They were released into the noise.

Families swarmed.

Hugs. Photos. Flowers. People calling names across the gym like the room could carry anything without dropping it.

Emily found her parents. Her mother hugged her hard enough that Emily's ribs protested. Her dad hugged her with a quick, firm squeeze like he didn't want to get emotional in public.

Kate hugged her too, brief but tight, and then immediately stepped back to look at her.

"Okay," Kate said. "Now you look like a graduate."

Emily blinked. "What did I look like before."

Kate shrugged. "Like you were waiting for something to grab you."

Emily's throat tightened. Because Kate wasn't wrong. Kate was never wrong.

Grandpa hugged her and said, "Proud of you," and it sounded like it meant more than grades.

Grandma hugged her last.

It wasn't a dramatic hug. It wasn't trembling. It wasn't some cinematic closure.

It was simply Grandma's arms around her, steady and careful and real.

And when she pulled back, Grandma's eyes were wet—but her voice was calm.

"You did good," she said.

Emily swallowed. "Yeah?"

Grandma nodded once. "Yeah."

Then she stepped away, like she'd given Emily what she could and wouldn't take up more space than she deserved.

Emily found Zoe near the side wall, already being cornered by a well-meaning adult.

"So where you headed?" the woman asked brightly.

Zoe smiled politely in the way she had mastered—sharp teeth hidden behind manners. "University of Montana," she said. "Pre-law."

The woman's eyes widened. "Oh! Wow. That's... big."

Zoe's smile didn't change. "Yes," she said. "That's the idea."

When the woman turned away, Zoe exhaled. "I'm going to miss being underestimated," she said.

Emily's mouth tilted. "No you're not."

Zoe looked at her. "Fair."

Blake came up behind Emily and slid his arm around her waist like it had been there for years. His mouth brushed her temple—brief, easy, not showy.

"Want out?" he murmured.

Emily nodded.

They drifted toward the gym doors as the crowd shifted around them. Not running. Not escaping. Just leaving the noise the way you left a room you'd been in long enough.

In the hallway, the air was cooler again.

The lockers were still. The baby photos smiled from the wall like proof that time was a trick.

Zoe fell into step beside them, cap in her hands like she hadn't decided what to do with it yet.

"So," Zoe said, voice dry, "are we doing the thing."

Emily looked at her. "What thing."

Zoe lifted her brows. "The post-graduation ritual where everyone drives somewhere scenic and pretends they're not terrified."

Blake snorted quietly. "That's pretty accurate."

Emily's phone buzzed in her hand.

Her phone buzzed.

Unknown Number: You don't need me anymore.

Emily's breath caught — not in fear, but recognition.

She didn't type back right away.

Then:

Unknown Number: Take what you're carrying. Go forward.

Emily locked the screen and slid her phone into her pocket like it couldn't burn through fabric.

Blake's hand tightened at her waist. "Lake?" he asked, like it was an answer and not a question.

Emily looked at Zoe.

Zoe sighed dramatically. "Fine. Yes. The lake. Because apparently none of you are capable of processing emotions without involving water."

Emily's laugh came out real this time—quick, surprised.

Kate's voice floated from the gym doorway behind them. "Where are you going?"

Emily turned.

Kate stood there with her sketchbook tucked under her arm, watching them like she was already composing the scene in her head.

Emily didn't lie. "Out," she said. "For a minute."

Kate nodded like she understood more than Emily had said. "Don't do anything illegal," she called.

Zoe looked back at her. "Define illegal."

Kate's mouth twitched. "You know what I mean."

Blake leaned in and kissed Emily—brief, light, familiar—and then stepped back like it was the easiest thing in the world.

"Text your mom," Zoe said to Emily. "So she doesn't send a search party."

Emily nodded and did it, quick.

Then the three of them walked out into the bright May afternoon, gowns still on, caps in hand, the sun too warm and the air too clean and the future too close to ignore.

They moved toward their vehicles without hurry.

Not because they weren't carrying anything.

Because they were.

And they were walking anyway.

CHAPTER FORTY NINE

The Edge

They rode together.

Blake drove. Emily sat in the middle without comment. Zoe climbed in last, tossing her cap onto the dash like she was finished negotiating with it.

No one asked where they were going.

The sky was so blue it almost hurt to look at—clean and stretched wide, the kind of blue that made you squint without realizing it. Emily had learned, over the past months, to notice when the world repeated itself too precisely.

It was the same blue it had been sixty years ago.

The truck rumbled out of town, familiar roads sliding beneath the tires. Fields blurred past, green and sharp-edged, the season confident in itself. Blake drove with one hand on the wheel, relaxed but attentive, like this stretch of road belonged to muscle memory more than thought.

Emily rested her hands in her lap and let the movement carry her.

Zoe leaned back against the door, gown pooled awkwardly around her knees. "I just want it on record," she said, "that if this becomes emotionally significant, I will complain the entire time."

Blake huffed. "You always do."

"Yes," Zoe said. "But with purpose."

Emily smiled, quiet and real.

They pulled into the overlook lot without stopping to assess it. No fence. No signs. The temporary barriers were gone, cleared away so efficiently it was almost like they'd never been there.

The lake lay below them, full now. Ordinary. Reflective. Innocent-looking, the way only water ever was.

They shut the doors and stood for a moment, adjusting.

The gowns made movement awkward—fabric catching at knees, sleeves shifting when arms lifted. Emily was aware of it, the way ceremony insisted on being carried even when the moment had already passed.

She walked first.

The path down was unchanged. Packed dirt. Loose stone. The slow descent toward something that didn't rush you.

At the edge, Emily stopped and slipped her shoes off, balancing briefly before setting her bare feet into the damp sand. Cold bit immediately, sharp enough to draw a breath from her chest.

She stepped forward anyway.

Zoe watched her, then sighed theatrically. "You're contagious." She kicked her shoes off and stepped beside her, shivering once. "I hate that this works."

Blake followed last, rolling his jeans once, then again, careful. When he stepped into the water, his breath left him slowly, like he was deciding not to react too much.

They stood there together.

The water lapped gently against their ankles, clear and cold and real. Emily stared out across the surface—no outlines, no shadows of what lay beneath.

Just sky reflected back at itself.

She let her shoulders drop.

Zoe broke the quiet first, softer now. "So this is it," she said. "Not closure. Just...placement."

Emily nodded. "Yeah."

Blake's hand found Emily's without ceremony. Their fingers fit easily, like they'd learned the shape of each other somewhere along the way.

Emily looked down and took hold of Zoe's hand. Zoe's eyes registered suspicion first, but softened quickly. She squeezed Emily's fingers.

They stood there longer than necessary.

Not waiting. Not searching.

Just letting the lake be what it was now—and knowing what it had been.

The sky stayed blue. Painfully so. Unchanged.

Eventually, Zoe stepped back, shaking the cold from her feet. "Okay," she said briskly. "I've respected the symbolism. I'm hungry."

Emily laughed.

They stepped back from the water together, shoes in hand, gowns brushing against bare legs, the fabric darkening slightly at the hems.

They didn't look back.

They didn't need to.

The lake held.

And they went on.

Thank You for Reading

Thank you for spending time in Evansville and for reading *What the Lake Knows*. Stories like this travel farthest through word of mouth, and readers like you make that possible.

If you enjoyed this novel, would you consider leaving a review on Goodreads? Even a brief review helps other readers discover the book and means more than you might realize.

You can also visit **www.devienneweekes.com** for reader resources, discussion questions, and updates about future books.

Thank you again for reading and for helping this story find its way to other readers.

— Devienne Weekes